Death of a Hawker

"As a microcosm of the western world, beset by riots, greed, get-rich-quick schemes, smoldering jealousy linking together men who were once close friends, Amsterdam is now the perfect crime setting. . . . [In *Death of a Hawker*] it is the subtle psychological probing that will sort it all out in the end, peeling off layers of pretension, showing how each member of the police team will react under pressure. A puzzle up to the very end."
—*Publishers Weekly*

Featuring
Grijpstra and de Gier

"What makes this series so engaging is that the policemen are as quirky and complicated and human as the criminals."
—*Washington Post*

"Offbeat, inventive"
—*Seattle Post-Intelligencer*

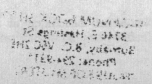

Books by Janwillem van de Wetering

The Empty Mirror
A Glimpse of Nothingness
Outsider in Amsterdam
Tumbleweed
The Corpse on the Dike
Death of a Hawker
The Japanese Corpse
The Blond Baboon

Published by POCKET BOOKS

DEATH
OF A HAWKER

Janwillem van de Wetering

PUBLISHED BY POCKET BOOKS NEW YORK

POCKET BOOKS, a Simòn & Schuster division of
GULF & WESTERN CORPORATION
1230 Avenue of the Americas, New York, N.Y. 10020

To
Lenore Straus

DEATH
OF A HAWKER

1

"YES, MADAM," the constable said quietly. "Would you mind telling me who you are? And where you are?"

"He is dead," the soft veiled voice said, "dead. He is on the floor. His head is all bloody. When I came into the room he was still breathing but now he is dead."

She had said it three times already.

"Yes, madam," the constable said again. There was patience in the way he said it, understanding. Love, perhaps. But the constable was acting. He had been well trained. He was only concerned about finding out who was speaking to him, and where she might be. The constable had been working in the central radio room of Amsterdam Police Headquarters for some years now. He took a lot of calls. Anybody who dials two six times gets through to the central radio room. Anybody means a lot of people. Some of them are serious citizens, some of them are mad. And some of them are temporarily mad. They have seen something, experienced a sensation. The experience may have knocked them free of their usual routine, perhaps to the point where

they are suffering from shock. Or they are drunk. Or
they just want to talk to someone, to know that they
are not alone, and there is someone amongst the million inhabitants of Holland's capital who cares enough
to listen. Someone who is alive, not just a taped voice
which tells them that God is Good and All is Well.

"You say he is dead," the constable said quietly. "I
am very sorry about that, but I can only come to see
you if I know where you are. I can help you, madam,
but where do you want me to go and look for you?
Where are you, madam?"

The constable wasn't planning to go to see the lady.
It was five o'clock in the afternoon and he would be
off duty in fifteen minutes. He was planning to go
home, have a meal and go to bed. He had put in a lot
of hours that day, many more than he was used to.
The central radio room was manned by a skeleton staff,
short of three senior constables and a sergeant. The
constable thought of his colleagues and smiled grimly.
He could picture them clearly enough, for he had
watched them leaving the large courtyard of Headquarters that morning. White-helmeted, carrying cane
shields and long leather sticks, part of one of the many
platoons which had roared off in blue armor-plated
vans. It was riot time in Amsterdam again. They hadn't
had riots for years now and the screaming mobs, flying
bricks, howling fanatics leading swaying crowds, exploding gas grenades, bleeding faces, the sirens of ambulances and police vehicles were almost forgotten.
Now it had started all over again. The constable had
volunteered for riot duty but someone had to man the
telephones, so he was still here, listening to the lady.
The lady expected him to come and see her. He wouldn't.
But once he knew where she was, a car would race out
and there would be policemen in the car and the lady
was now speaking to the police. Police are police.

The constable was looking at his form. Name and a
dotted line. Address, and a dotted line. Subject, dead
man. Time, 1700 hours. She had probably gone up to
call the dead man for tea, or an early dinner. She had

called him from the corridor, or the dining room. He hadn't answered. So she had gone up to his room.

"Your name, please, madam," the constable said again. His voice hadn't changed. He wasn't hurrying her.

"Esther Rogge," the woman said.

"Your address, madam?"

"Straight Tree Ditch Four."

"Who is the dead man, madam?"

"My brother Abe."

"You are sure he is dead, madam?"

"Yes. He is dead. He is on the floor. His head is all bloody." She had said it before.

"Right," the constable said briskly. "We'll be right there, madam. Don't worry about a thing now, madam. We'll be right there."

The constable slipped the little form through a hole in the glass window which separated him from the radio operator. He waved at the operator. The operator nodded, shoving two other forms aside.

"Three one," the operator said.

"Three one," Detective-Sergeant de Gier said.

"Straight Tree Ditch Four. Dead man. Bloody head. Name is Abe Rogge. Ask for his sister, Esther Rogge. Over."

Sergeant de Gier looked at the little loudspeaker underneath the dashboard of the gray VW he was driving.

"Straight Tree Ditch?" he asked in a high voice. "How do you expect me to get there? There are thousands of people milling about in the area. Haven't you heard about the riots?"

The operator shrugged.

"Are you there?" de Gier asked.

"I am here," the operator said. "Just go there. The death has nothing to do with the riots, I think."

"Right," de Gier said, still in the same high voice.

"Good luck," the operator said. "Out."

De Gier accelerated and Adjutant-Detective Grijpstra sat up.

"Easy," Grijpstra said. "We are in an unmarked car and that traffic light is on red. They should have sent a marked car, a car with a siren."

"I don't think there are any left," de Gier said, and stopped at the traffic light. "Everybody is out there, everybody we know and a lot of military police as well. I haven't seen a police car all day." He sighed. "The crowd will clobber us the minute they see us go through the roadblocks."

The light changed and the car shot off.

"Easy," Grijpstra said.

"No," de Gier said. "Let's go home. This isn't the right day to play detectives."

Grijpstra grinned and shifted his heavy body into a more comfortable position, holding on to the car's roof and the dashboard at the same time. "You are all right," he said. "You don't look like a policeman. They'll go for me. Crowds always go for me."

De Gier took a corner and avoided a parked truck by forcing the VW's right wheels onto the sidewalk. They were in a narrow alley leading to the Newmarket, the center of the riots. Nobody was about. The riots had sucked people into their vortex while others stayed inside, preferring the small rooms of their seventeenth-century homes to the raw danger of violent hysteria which stalked the streets, changing apparently normal people into robots swinging fists and primitive weapons, intent on attacking and destroying the State which, through their bloodshot and bulging eyes, showed itself as the Police, rows and rows of blue-uniformed and white-helmeted warriors, nonhuman, machines of oppression. They saw the riot police guarding the exit of the alley and a commanding gloved hand was raised to stop the car. De Gier turned his window down and showed his card.

The face under the helmet was unfamiliar and de Gier could read the words on the badge pinned on the man's jacket. "THE HAGUE," the badge said.

"You from The Hague?" de Gier asked, surprised.

"Yes, sergeant, there are about fifty of us here. We were rushed in this morning."

"Police from The Hague," de Gier said surprised. "What next?"

"Rotterdam, I suppose," the constable said. "There are plenty of cities in Holland. We'll all come and help you on a nice day like this. Just give the word. You want to go through?"

"Yes," de Gier said. "We are supposed to investigate a manslaughter on the other side of the square."

The constable shook his head. "I'll let you through but you'll get stuck anyway. The water cannon has just charged the crowd and they are in a foul mood now. One of my colleagues has caught a brick full in the face and they rushed him when he fell. We got him to the ambulance just in time. Maybe you should try to get there on foot."

De Gier turned and looked at Grijpstra, who smiled reassuringly. Inspired by his superior's calm, de Gier nodded at the constable. "We'll park her here."

"Right," the constable said, and turned. The crowd was coming their way, pushed by a charge of unseen policemen on the other side of the square. The constable braced himself, raising his shield to ward off a brick, a heavy man suddenly lurched forward and the constable hit him on the shoulder with his stick. The blow made a dull sound and the heavy man faltered. There were a dozen policemen between the detectives and the crowd now and Grijpstra pulled de Gier onto a porch.

"We may as well wait for the fight to shift."

Together they watched a brick dent the roof of their car.

"Cigar?" Grijpstra asked.

De Gier shook his head and began to roll a cigarette. His hands trembled. What on earth inspired these people? He knew about the official causes of the riots, everybody knew. The underground, Amsterdam's new means of transport, had tunneled as far as this old and protected part of the inner city and some houses had to come down to make way for the monster eating its way through down below. There would be a station here sometime in the future. Most of Amsterdam accepted the underground; it had to come, to relieve the impossible traffic trying to get through the narrow streets and fouling the air. But the inhabitants of the Newmarket area had put up a protest. They wanted the station to be built somewhere else. They had written to the mayor, they had marched through the city, they had printed tens of thousands of posters and pasted them up everywhere, they had harassed the offices of the Public Works Department. And the mayor and his aldermen had tried to appease the protests. They had said "yes" sometimes and "no" at other times. And then, one day, the demolishing firm that had won the city's contract suddenly arrived and began to tear at the houses, and the citizens had fought with the wreckers and chased them off and had grappled, successfully at first, with the police.

Now the wreckers were back and the police had come out in force. The citizens would lose, of course. But meanwhile they were organized. They had bought two-way radios and put up guard posts. They had coordinated their defense and thrown up barricades. They were wearing motorcycle helmets and had armed themselves with sticks. They were even supposed to have armored trucks. But why? They would lose anyway.

Grijpstra, sucking at his small cigar, listened to the growling of the mob. The mob was very close now, its snout no farther away than ten feet. The policemen were holding their ground, being reinforced by a squad which had rushed up through the alley. Three constables had stopped when they saw the two civilians hiding on the porch but Grijpstra's police card had sent them on their way again.

Why? Grijpstra thought, but he knew the answer. This wasn't just a protest against the building of an underground station. There had always been violence in the city. Amsterdam, by its tolerance for unconventional behavior, attracts crazy people. Holland is a conventional country; crazy people have to go somewhere.

They go to the capital, where the lovely canals, thousands and thousands of gable houses, hundreds of bridges of every shape and form, lines of old trees, clusters of offbeat bars and cafés, dozens of small cinemas and theaters encourage and protect the odd. Crazy people are special people. They carry the country's genius, its urge to create, to find new ways. The State smiles and is proud of its crazy people. But the State does not approve of anarchism. It limits the odd.

The Newmarket area is very odd. And now, when the odd tried to argue with the State's choice of an underground station, and lost the argument, and reverted to violence, the State lost its smile and produced its strength, the strength of the blue-uniformed city police, and the black-uniformed military police, resplendent with white and silver braid, and reinforced with steel helmets and truncheons, and backed with armored cars and mechanical carriers equipped with water guns, spouting thousands of gallons of pressurized water on and against the bearded yelling hooligans who, only this morning, were artists and artisans, poets or unemployed intellectuals, gentle misfits and innocent dreamers.

De Gier sighed. A paper bag filled with powdered soapstone had flown into the alley and exploded on the pavement. The right side of his stylish suit, made out of blue denim by a cheap Turkish tailor, was stained with the white sticky substance. De Gier was an elegant man who took pride in his appearance. He was also a handsome man and he didn't like the feel of the powder in his mustache. Some of it would be on his thick curly hair. He didn't relish the idea of having a white mustache for the rest of the day. Grijpstra laughed.

"You caught some of it too," de Gier said.

Grijpstra looked at his trousers but he didn't care. All his suits were the same, baggy and made of English striped material, thin white stripes on a blue background. The suit was old, like the gray tie, and he wouldn't mourn its loss. His shirt was new but the police

would replace it if he filled in a report. Grijpstra leaned
back against the door at the back of the porch and
placed his hands on his stomach. He looked very placid.

"We ought to try and get through," de Gier said.
"That lady will be waiting for us."

"In a minute," Grijpstra said. "If we try now we'll
only be food for the ambulance. If the hooligans don't
get us the police will. They won't take the time to study
our cards. They'll be nervous as well."

De Gier smoked and listened. The fight had moved,
it seemed. The screams and thuds were a little farther
away now.

"Now," he said, and stepped into the alley. The constables let them through. They ran across the square
and dodged a heavy motorcycle and sidecar which came
straight at them. The sergeant in the sidecar was beating the metal side of his vehicle with his rubber stick.
His face had been cut by a woman's nails and blood
had run all over his tunic. The constable driving the
contraption was gray with dust and sweat streaked his
face.

"Police," Grijpstra boomed.

The motorcycle veered and charged the mob which
had begun to form again behind the detectives.

Grijpstra fell. Two boys, in their late teens, had
heard him shout "Police" and they both attacked at the
same time, kicking the adjutant's shins. De Gier was
quick, but not quick enough. He hit the nearest boy on
the side of the chin and the boy sighed and crumpled
up. The other boy had been hit with the same movement, not by de Gier's fist but by his elbow. The elbow's
sharp point hit the boy on the side of his face and he
howled with pain and ran off.

"All right?" de Gier asked, helping Grijpstra back to
his feet.

They ran on but an armored van was in their way
now and a spout of water hit them from behind. De
Gier fell. Now the water gun changed its position, and
was aiming at Grijpstra's large bulk when the gunner

saw the red stripes on the police card which the adjutant waved.

"Go away," a police officer shouted at the detectives. "What the hell do you think you are doing here? We don't want any plainclothesmen around."

"Sorry, sir," Grijpstra said. "We have a call from the Straight Tree Ditch; this is the only way to get there."

"Let them wait," the inspector roared, his young face pale with fear.

"Can't. Manslaughter."

"All right, all right. I'll give you an escort although I can't spare anyone. Hey! You and you. Take these men through. They are ours."

Two burly military policemen answered the command, both with torn braid dangling from their shoulders.

"Shit," the nearest of the two said. "We have had everything today short of gunfire and we'll have that too if this goes on much longer."

"Nobody went for his gun so far?" Grijpstra asked.

"One of your young chappies did," the military policeman said, "but we quieted him down. His mate had caught a brick in the face. Upset him a bit. Had to take the gun away from him in the end; said he would shoot the fellow who got his mate."

Grijpstra meant to say something positive but a bag of soapstone powder hit them and he couldn't see for a while.

"Messy, hey?" the military policeman said. "They must have tons of that damned powder. We caught a man on the roof using a heavy catapult; he was our first prisoner. I'd like to see the charge report we'll come up with. It will be crossbows next and mechanical stone throwers. Have you seen their armored trucks?"

"No," de Gier said. "Where?"

"We got them early fortunately, two of them. There's nothing you can do when they come at you. Friend of mine jumped straight into the canal to get away. The crowd was very amused."

"Did you catch the driver?"

"Sure. Pulled him out of the cabin myself, had to smash the window for he had locked himself in. That's one report I am going to write myself. He'll get three months."

"Nice day," Grijpstra said. "Let's go. We have a lady waiting for us."

They got to the lady ten minutes later. They only got into one more fight. Grijpstra was bitten in the hand. De Gier pulled the woman off by the hair. The military policemen arrested the woman. Her artificial teeth fell out as they threw her into a van. They picked up the teeth and threw them in after her.

2

THE STRAIGHT TREE DITCH is a narrow canal flanked
by two narrow quays and shadowed by lines of elm
trees which, on that spring evening, filtered the light
through their haze of fresh pale green leaves. Its lovely
old houses, supporting each other in their great age,
mirror themselves in the canal's water, and any tourist
who strays off the beaten track and suddenly finds himself in the centuries-old peace of this secluded spot will
agree that Amsterdam has a genuine claim to beauty.

But our detectives were in no mood to appreciate
beauty. Grijpstra's shins hurt him and the wound on his
hand was ugly. His short bristly hair was white with
soapstone powder and his jacket had been torn by an
assailant whom he had never noticed. De Gier limped
next to him and snarled at a policeman who told them
to be off. There were no civilians about, for the canal
offered no room for mobs, but the police had sealed its
entrance to prevent access to the Newmarket Square.
Red and white wooden fences had been hastily installed
and riot police guarded the roadblocks, staring at the

curious, who, silently, stood and stared back. There
was nothing to see, the fighting in the square being
screened by high gable houses. The atmosphere of the
canal was heavy, loaded with violence and suspicion,
and the policemen, forced into idleness, hit their high
leather boots with their truncheons, splitting the silence.
Far away the revving engines of motorcycles and trucks
could be heard, and the whining of the water cannon,
and the subdued yells of the combatants, eerily setting
off the clamor of machines. Demolition was still continuing, for the houses had to come down, the sooner
the better, and the cranes, bulldozers and automatic
steel hammers and drills were adding their racket to
the general upheaval.

"We are police, buddy," de Gier said to the cop, and
showed his card, which had got cracked when he fell.

"Sorry, sergeant," the constable said, "we trust nobody today. How is it going out there?"

"We are winning," Grijpstra said.

"We always win," the constable said. "It's boring,
I'd rather watch football."

"Number four," de Gier said. "Here we are."

The constable wandered off, hitting the canal's cast-
iron railing with his stick, and Grijpstra looked up at
the four-storied house, which was number four according to a neatly painted sign next to the front door.
"Rogge," said another sign.

"Took us three quarters of an hour to get here," de
Gier said. "Marvelous service we are giving nowadays,
and there's supposed to be a dead man with a bloody
face in there."

"Maybe not," Grijpstra said. "People exaggerate, you
know. Adjutant Geurts was telling me that he was called
to investigate a suicide last night and when he got to
the address the old lady was eating nice fresh toast with
a raw herring spread on top of it, and there were
chopped onions on top of the herring. She had changed
her mind. Life wasn't so bad after all."

"A man with a bloody head can't change his mind,"
de Gier said.

Grijpstra nodded. "True. And he won't be a suicide."

He rang the bell. There was no answer. He rang again. The door opened. The corridor was dark and they couldn't see the woman until the door had closed behind them.

"Upstairs," the woman said. "I'll go first."

They turned into another corridor on the second floor and the woman opened a door leading to a room facing the canal. The man was lying on his back on the floor, his face smashed.

"Dead," the woman said. "He was my brother, Abe Rogge."

Grijpstra pushed the woman gently aside and stooped to look at the dead man's face. "You know what happened?" he asked. The woman covered her face with her hands. Grijpstra put his arm around her shoulders. "Do you know anything, miss?" "No, no. I came in and there he was."

Grijpstra looked at de Gier and pointed at a telephone with his free hand. De Gier dialed. Grijpstra pulled his arm back from the woman's shoulders and took the telephone from de Gier's limp hand.

"Take her outside," he whispered, "and don't look at the body. You two have some coffee, I saw a kitchen downstairs; I'll see you there later."

De Gier was white in the face when he led the woman outside. He had to support himself against the doorpost. Grijpstra smiled. He had seen it before. The sergeant was allergic to blood, but he would be all right soon.

"The man's head is bashed in," he said on the phone. "Do what you have to do and get us the commissaris."

"You are in the riot area, aren't you?" the central radio room asked. "We'll never get the cars through."

"Get a launch from the State Water Police," Grijpstra said. "That's what we should have had. Don't forget to get the commissaris. He is at home."

He replaced the phone and put his hands into his pockets. The windows of the room were open and the elm trees outside screened the pale blue sky. He looked at their leaves for a while, resting his eyes on their delicate young green and admiring a blackbird which, unperturbed by the weird atmosphere of his surroundings, had burst into song. A sparrow hopped about on the windowsill and looked at the corpse, its tiny head cocked to one side. Grijpstra walked over to the window. The blackbird and the sparrow flew off but gulls continued swooping down toward the canal's surface, looking for scraps and dead fish. It was the beginning of a spring evening which the occupant of the room would have no part of.

How? Grijpstra thought. The man's face was a mess of broken bones and thick bright red blood. A big man, some thirty years old perhaps. The body was dressed in jeans and a blue bush jacket. There was a thick golden necklace around the muscular neck and its skin was tanned. He has been on holiday, Grijpstra thought, just returned probably. Spain. North Africa perhaps, or an island somewhere. Must have been in the sun for weeks. Nobody gets a tan from the Dutch spring.

He noted the short yellow curls, bleached by exposure, and the beard of exactly the same texture. The hair fitted the man's head like a helmet. Strong fellow, Grijpstra thought, could lift a horse off the ground. Heavy wrists, bulging arms.

He squatted down, looked at the man's face again and then began to look around the room. Not seeing what he was looking for, he began to walk around, carefully, his hands still in his pockets. But the brick or stone wasn't there. It had seemed such a simple straightforward solution. Man looks out of the window. Riot outside. Someone flings a brick. Brick hits man in the face. Man falls over backward. Brick falls in the room. But there was no brick. He walked to the window and looked down into the street. He still couldn't see a brick. The helmeted policeman who had stopped them earlier was leaning against a tree staring at the water.

"Hey, you," Grijpstra shouted. The policeman looked up. "Has there been any stone throwing here this afternoon?"

"No," the constable shouted back. "Why?"

"Chap here has his face smashed in, could have been a stone."

The constable scratched his neck. "I'll go and ask the others," he shouted after a while. "I haven't been here all afternoon."

"The stone may have bounced off this man's face here and fallen back into the street. Get some of your friends, please, and search the street, will you?"

The constable waved and ran off. Grijpstra turned around. It could have been a weapon, of course, or perhaps even a fist. Several blows perhaps. No knife. A hammer? A hammer perhaps, Grijpstra thought, and sat down on the only chair he saw, a large cane chair with a high back. He had seen a similar chair in a shop window some days before and he remembered the price. A high price. The table in the room was expensive as well, antique and heavily built with a single ornamental leg. There was a book on the table, a French book. Grijpstra read the title. *Zazie dans le Métro*. It had a picture of a little girl on the cover. Some little girl having an adventure on the underground. Grijpstra didn't read French. There wasn't much more to see in the room. A low table with a telephone, a telephone directory and some more French books in a heap on the floor. The walls of the room had been left bare, with the exception of one fairly large unframed painting. He studied the painting with interest. It took him a while to name what he saw. The picture seemed to consist of no more than a large black dot, or a constellation of dots against a background of blues, but it had to be a boat, he decided in the end. A small boat, a canoe or a dinghy, afloat on a fluorescent sea. And there were two men in the boat. The painting wasn't as sad as it seemed at first glance. The fluorescence of the sea, indicated by stripes of white along the boat, and continuing into its wake, suggested some gaiety. The painting impressed him and he kept on looking back at it. Other objects in the room held his attention for a moment but the painting drew him back. If the corpse hadn't been there, dominating the space by its awkward and grotesque presence, the room would have been a perfect setting for the painting. Grijpstra himself had some talent and he meant to paint seriously one day. He had painted as a young man, but marriage and the family which suddenly began to spread around him, and the small uncomfortable house on the Lijnbaans- gracht opposite Police Headquarters, drowned in the holocaust of a TV which his deaf wife would never switch off, and the fat ever-present existence of the flabby woman who shouted at him and the children had frustrated and almost killed his ambition. How would he paint a small boat, afloat on its own on an immense sea? He would use more color, Grijpstra thought, but more color would spoil the dream. For the picture was a dream, a dream dreamed simultaneously by two friends, two men suspended in space, drawn as two small interlinked line structures.

He stretched his legs, leaned back and breathed heavily. This would be a room he could live in. Life would become a pleasure, for a hard day would never be a hard day if he knew he could return to this room. And the dead man had lived in this room. He sighed again; the sigh tapered off into a low groan. He looked at the low bed close to the window. There were three sleeping bags on the bed, one zipped and two unzipped. The man would have slept in the one bag and have used the other two for cover in case he needed it. Very sensible. No fuss with sheets. If a man wants sheets he needs a woman. The woman has to make the bed and change the sheets and take care of the other hundred thousand things a man thinks he needs.

Grijpstra would like to sleep on a stretcher and cover himself with an unzipped sleeping bag. In the morning he gets up and leaves the bed as it is. No vacuum cleaner. Sweep the room once a week. No TV. No newspapers. Just a few books maybe and a few records, not too many. Don't buy anything. Whatever you attract clut- ters up your life. He might invite a woman to the room, of course, but only if he could be absolutely sure that

she would leave again, and would never stick plastic
pins into her hair and sleep with them on. He felt his
face. There was a scratch which had got there before
he had fought his way through the riot. Mrs. Grijpstra
had ripped his face with one of her pins; she had turned
over and he had screamed with pain but she hadn't
awakened. His scream had stopped her snore halfway
and she had smacked her lips a few times and finished
the snore. And when he had shaken her by the shoulder
she had opened one bleary eye and told him to shut up.
And no children. There are enough children in Holland.

"Why the hell . . ." he said aloud now but he didn't
bother to finish the question. He had slipped into the
mess so gradually that he had never been able to stop
and twist free. The girl had looked all right when he
stumbled across her path, and her parents too, and he
was making a bit of a career in the police, and it was
all dead right. His oldest son had gradually grown into
a lout, with long dirty straight hair and buck teeth and
a shiny screaming motorcycle. The two little ones were
still very nice. He loved them. No doubt about it. He
wouldn't leave them. So he couldn't have a room like
this. All very logical. He looked at the corpse again. Had
someone come in and hit the giant with a hammer,
smack in the face? And had the giant stood there, seeing the hammer come and catching its impact full on
the nose, without even trying to defend himself? Drunk
perhaps? He got up and went over to the window.
Three constables were poking at the cobblestones with
their long truncheons.

"Anything there?"

They looked up. "Nothing."

"Did you find out about the stone throwing?"

"Yes," the constable who had been there earlier
shouted back. "It has been quiet here all day. We were
only here to stop people getting to the trouble spot."

"Have you let anyone through?"

The constables looked at each other, then the first
one looked up at Grijpstra again.

"Plenty. Anybody who had business here."

"A man has been killed here," Grijpstra shouted. "Have you noticed anyone running about? Behaving in a funny way?"

The constables shook their heads.

"Thanks," Grijpstra shouted and pulled his head in. He sat down again and closed his eyes, meaning to feel the atmosphere of the room but gradually drifting off into sleep. The sound of a ship's engine woke him. He looked out and saw a low launch of the Water Police moor outside. Some six men got off, the commissaris, a small dapper-looking elderly man first. Grijpstra waved and the men marched up to the door.

"Nice coffee." de Gier had been saying meanwhile. "Thank you very much. Drink some yourself, you need it. Please tell me what happened. Are you all right now?"

The woman sitting opposite him at the kitchen table tried to smile. A slender woman with dark hair, done up in a bun, and dressed in black slacks and a black blouse with a necklace of small red shells. She wore no rings.

"I am his sister," she said. "Esther Rogge. Call me Esther, please, everybody does. We have lived here for five years now. I used to have a flat but Abe bought this house and wanted me to move in with him."

"Looked after your brother," de Gier said. "I see."

"No. Abe didn't need anyone to look after him. We just shared the house. I have the first floor, he has the second. We hardly ever even ate together."

"Why not?" de Gier asked, lighting her cigarette. She had long hands, no lacquer on the nails, one nail was broken.

"We preferred not to fuss with each other. Abe kept the refrigerator stocked and he just ate what he liked. If we happened to be both in I might cook something for him but he would never ask me to. He often ate out. We lived our own lives."

"What did he do for a living?" de Gier asked.

Esther tried to smile again. Her face was still white

and the shadows under her eyes showed up as dark purple stains but some life had returned to her mouth, which was no longer a slit in a mask.

"He was a hawker, sold things in the street. In the street market, the Albert Cuyp Market. You know the Albert Cuyp, of course?"

"Yes, miss."

"Please call me Esther. I sometimes went to see him in the Albert Cuyp. I have helped him too when I had a day off. He sold beads, and all types of cloth, and wool and colored string and braid. To people who like to make things themselves."

"Creative," de Gier said.

"Yes. It's fashionable to be creative now."

"You say your brother bought this house? Must have cost him some money or did he get a substantial mortgage?"

"No, it's all his. He made a lot of money. He wasn't just selling things in the street, you see, he dealt in a big way as well. He was always going to Czechoslovakia in a van and he would buy beads by the ton, directly from the factory, and he would sell to other hawkers and to the big stores too. And he bought and sold other things as well. The street market was for fun, he only went there on Mondays."

"And you, what do you do?"

"I work for the university, I have a degree in literature." De Gier looked impressed.

"What's your name?" Esther asked.

"De Gier. Detective-Sergeant de Gier. Rinus de Gier."

"May I call you Rinus?"

"Please," de Gier said, and poured himself more coffee. "Do you have any idea why this happened? Any connection with the riots, you think?"

"No," she said. Her eyes filled with tears and de Gier reached out and held her hand.

"They threw something at him," the commissaris said, looking down at the corpse. "With force, considerable

force. From the impact you would almost think they
shot something at him. A stone perhaps. But where is
it?"

Grijpstra explained what he had been able to deduct
from his investigations so far.

"I see," the commissaris said pensively. "No stone,
you say. And no bits of brick, I see. They were throwing bricks on the Newmarket Square, I am told. Red
bricks. They break and pulverize when they hit something. There is no red dust on the floor here. Could
have been a proper stone though and somebody may
have found it and thrown it into the canal."

"There would have been a splash, sir, and the street
has been patrolled all day."

The commissaris laughed. "Yes. Manslaughter and
we are sitting right on top of it, have been sitting on it
all day, and we never noticed. Peculiar, isn't it?"

"Yes, sir."

"And he can't have been dead long. Hours, no more.
A few hours, I would say. The doctor'll be here in a
minute, the launch has gone back to pick him up. He'll
know. Where's de Gier?"

"Downstairs, sir, talking to the man's sister."

"Couldn't stand the blood, could he? You think he'll
ever get used to it?"

"No sir, not if he is forced to look at it for some
time. We were in the middle of the riot and he put up
a good fight and he didn't mind the blood on my hand
but if blood is combined with death it seems to get
him. Makes him vomit. I sent him down just in time."

"Every man has his own fear," the commissaris said
softly. "But what caused all this, I wonder? Can't have
been a bullet for there is no hole, but every bone in the
face seems to have been smashed. Hey! Who are you?"

He had seen a man walking past the door in the
corridor, a young man who now entered the room.

"Louis Zilver," the young man said.

"What are you doing here?"

"I live here, I have a room upstairs."

"We are policemen investigating the death of Mr.

Rogge here. Can we come to your room? The photographers and print people will want to have a look at this room and we can use the opportunity to ask a few questions."

"Certainly," the young man said.

They followed Zilver up a flight of narrow stairs and were shown into a large room. The commissaris took the only easy chair, Grijpstra sat on the bed, the young man sat on the floor, facing them both.

"I am a friend of Abe and Esther," Louis said. "I have been living in this house for almost a year now."

"Go ahead," the commissaris said. "Tell us all you know. About the house, about what went on, about what everybody does. We know nothing. We have just come in. But first of all I would like you to tell me if you know how Abe died and where you were at the time."

"I was here," Louis said. "I have been in the house all day. Abe was still alive at four o'clock this afternoon. He was here then, right here in this room. And I don't know how he died."

"Go on," the commissaris said pleasantly.

3

Louis Zilver's room was almost as bare as the dead man's room one floor below, but it had a different quality. The commissaris, who hadn't spent as much time with Abe Rogge's body as Grijpstra had, didn't notice the difference. He just saw another room in the same house, a room with a bare wooden floor and furnished with a neatly made bed and a large desk, cylinder-topped, showing an array of cubicles, stacked with papers in plastic transparent folders, and a bookcase covering an entire wall. Grijpstra defined the difference as a difference between "neat" and "untidy." Zilver had to be an organized man, or boy rather, for he wouldn't be much older than twenty. Grijpstra observed Louis, squatting patiently opposite his interrogators, and noted the large, almost liquid, dark eyes, the delicately hooked nose, the tinge of olive in the color of the skin stretched over high cheekbones, the long blue-black hair. Louis was waiting. Meanwhile he wasn't doing much. He had crossed his legs and lit a cigarette after placing an ashtray in a convenient place so that the commissaris and

Grijpstra could tip the ash of their small cigars into it. The ashtray fascinated Grijpstra. It was a human skull, molded in plastic, a large hole had been left in the cranium and a silver cup fitted into the hole.

"Brr," Grijpstra said. "Some ashtray!"

Louis smiled. The smile was arrogant, condescending. "Friend of mine made it. He is a sculptor. Silly thing really, but it's useful so I kept it. And the meaning is obvious. Memento mori."

"Why do you have it if you think it's silly" the commissaris asked. "You could have thrown it out and used a saucer instead." The commissaris, who had spent the day in bed to ease the pain in his legs which had almost lamed him during the last few weeks, was rubbing his right leg. The hot needle pricks of his acute chronic rheumatism made his bloodless lips twitch. The commissaris looked very innocent. His shantung suit, complete with waistcoat and watch chain, seemed a little too large for his small dry body, and his wizened face with the carefully brushed, thin colorless hair expressed a gentle exactness.

"The man is a friend of mine, he often comes here. I think it would hurt him if I wasn't using his work of art. Besides, I don't mind having it around. The message of the skull may be obvious but it's true nevertheless. Life is short, seize the day and all that."

"Yes," the commissaris said. "There is a dead man in the house to prove the saying's worth."

The commissaris stopped to listen to the noises downstairs. Feet were clomping up and down the bare steps. The photographers would be setting up their equipment and the doctor would be getting ready to start his examination. A uniformed chief inspector, his jacket soaked and caked with soapstone powder, stomped his way into the room. The commissaris got up.

"Sir," the chief inspector said. "Anything we can do for you?"

"You have done enough today it seems," the commissaris said mildly.

"We haven't had any dead men outside," the chief inspector said. "Not so far, anyway."

"We have one here, one floor below. Got his face bashed in, hit by a stone or something, but we can't find the stone or whatever it was in his room."

"So my constables were telling me. Maybe your man was a reactionary, somebody the red mob outside may have disliked."

"Was he?" the commissaris asked Louis Zilver.

Louis grinned.

"Was he?"

"No," Louis said, carefully stubbing out his cigarette in the skull's silver cranium. "Abe didn't know what politics were. He was an adventurer."

"Adventurers get killed for a number of reasons," the chief inspector said, impatiently tapping his boot with his truncheon. "Do you have any use for me, sir?"

"No," the commissaris said, "no, you go ahead, I hope the situation is getting a bit better on the square."

"It isn't," the officer said. "It's getting worse. We are getting fresh crowds now, young idiots who come in screaming and dancing. I better get back."

Grijpstra watched Louis's face as the officer left the room. Louis was showing his teeth in the way a baboon does when he feels threatened. "It seems you are enjoying yourself," Grijpstra said.

"It's always nice to see the police get a beating," Louis said in a low voice.

Grijpstra bristled. The commissaris made a gesture. "Let's forget the Newmarket for a while. Tell us about the incident in this house. What do you know about it?"

Louis had lit a new cigarette and puffed industriously. "Esther found the body close to five o'clock this afternoon. She screamed. I was here, in my room. I ran downstairs. I told her to phone the police. Abe had been in my room an hour before Esther found him. He was right here, talking to me. There was nothing wrong with him then."

"What's your connection with Abe and Esther?"

"I am a friend. I got to know him on the market, the

Albert Cuyp Market. I bought a lot of beads from him once, kept on going back for more. I was trying to make a structure, an abstract figure which I was planning to hang from the ceiling. Abe was interested in what I was doing and came to see me where I lived. I had an uncomfortable room, small, no conveniences, no proper light. He was buying this house and suggested I move in with him. And we used to go sailing together. His boat is outside, moored next to that big houseboat you can see from the window. A clapped-out little yacht. He would take it out when there was a good wind but he found it difficult to handle by himself."

The commissaris and Grijpstra got up to look out of the window. They saw the sixteen-foot plastic sailboat.

"It's half full of water," Grijpstra said.

"Yes. Rainwater. He never bothered, just hosed it out when he wanted to go sailing. The sails are downstairs; it only takes a few minutes to rig the boat."

"What about that houseboat?"

"It's empty," Louis said. "Been for sale for a long time. They want too much money for it and it's rotten."

"Somebody could have stood on the roof and thrown whatever it was that hit Abe," the commissaris said thoughtfully. "Why don't you go down, Grijpstra? Perhaps the police in the street saw somebody on the houseboat."

"What was that nasty remark you made about the police just now?" the commissaris asked when Grijpstra had left the room. "You told Esther to telephone us when the body was found, didn't you? So we must be useful, why sneer at something which is useful?"

"The body had to be taken care of, hadn't it?" Louis asked, and his eyes sparkled. "We couldn't dump it into the canal, it would foul the water."

"I see. So you called the garbage men?" Louis dropped his eyes.

"But your friend is dead, his face is bashed in. Don't you want us to apprehend the killer?" Louis's face changed. It lost its sparkle and suddenly looked worn

and tired. The sensitive face became a study in sadness
only kept alive by the luster of the large eyes.

"Yes," Louis said softly. "He is dead, and we are
alone."

"We?"

"Esther, me, others, the people he inspired."

"Did he have enemies?"

"No. Friends. Friends and admirers. A lot of people
used to come and see him here. He threw parties and
they would do anything to be invited. He had lots of
friends."

"And in business? Was he popular in business as
well?"

"Yes," Louis said, staring at the plastic skull in front
of him. "King of the Albert Cuyp street market. Very
popular. All the street sellers knew him. Bought from
him too. He was a big businessman you know. We used
to bring in cargoes from Eastern Europe and a lot of it
was sold to the market. Lately we were doing wool,
tons of wool, for knitting and rug making. Wool is expensive stuff nowadays."

"We?" the commissaris asked.

"Well, Abe mostly. I just helped."

"Tell us about yourself."

"Why?"

"It may help us to understand the situation."

Louis grinned. "Yes, you are the police. I had almost
forgotten. But why should I help the police?"

Grijpstra had slipped into the room and taken his
place on the bed again. "You should help the police
because you are a citizen," Grijpstra boomed suddenly,
"because you are a member of society. Society can only
function when there is public order. When order has
been disturbed it has to be maintained again. It can
only be maintained if the citizens assist the police. The
task of the police is to protect the citizens against themselves."

Louis looked up and laughed.

"You think that's funny?" Grijpstra asked indignant-
ly.

"Yes. Very funny. Textbook phrases. And untrue. Why should I, a citizen, benefit by what you, in your stupidity, in your refusal to think, call public order? Couldn't it be that public order is sheer boredom, a heavy weight which throttles the citizens?"

"Your friend is dead downstairs, with a bashed-in face. Does that make you happy?"

Louis stopped laughing.

"You are a student, aren't you?" the commissaris asked.

"Yes. I studied law but I gave it up when I saw how sickening our laws are. I passed my candidate's examinations but that was as far as I could go, I haven't been near the university since."

"What a pity," the commissaris said. "I studied law too and I found it a fascinating discipline. You only have a few years to go. You don't want to finish your studies?"

The boy shrugged. "Why should I? If I become a master at law I may find myself in a concrete office somewhere working for some large company or perhaps even the State. I don't particularly want to join the establishment. It's more fun shouting at the street market or driving a truck through the snow in Czechoslovakia. And I am not after money."

"What would you do," Grijpstra asked, "if somebody rolled your wallet?"

"I wouldn't go to the police if that's what you mean."

"And if someone murdered your friend? Didn't you tell Esther to phone us?"

Louis sat up. "Listen," he said loudly. "Don't philosophize with me, will you? I am not used to arguing. I accept your power and your attempt to maintain order in a madhouse and I'll answer any questions you may ask as long as they relate to the murder."

"You mean that humanity consists of mindless forms groping about?" the commissaris asked dreamily as if he hadn't really been listening. He was looking at the trees outside the window.

"Yes, you've put it very well. We don't do anything,

things happen to us. Abe has found his death just now, like a few million black people have found their death in Central Africa because the water ran out. There's nothing anybody can do about it. My grandparents were thrown in a cattle truck during the war and dumped into some camp and gassed. Or maybe they just starved to death, or some SS man bashed their heads in for fun. Same thing happened to Abe and Esther's family. The Rogges stayed alive because they happened to survive; their lives weren't planned, like the deaths of the others weren't planned. And the police are pawns in the game. My grandparents were arrested by the police because they were Jews. By the Amsterdam municipal police, not the German police. They were told to maintain order, like you are now told to maintain order. That officer who was here a minute ago is merrily bashing heads now, on the Newmarket Square, half a kilometer from here."

"Really," Grijpstra said.

"What do you mean, *really?*" Louis shouted. "Are you going to tell me that only part of the police worked for the Germans during the war? And that most of your colleagues were on the queen's side? And what about the queen? Didn't she send troops to Indonesia to bash villagers on the head? What will you do if there's another war? Or a famine? It may happen any minute now." He coughed and looked at Grijpstra's face, ominously, as if he wanted the adjutant to agree with him.

"Or the Russians may invade us and impose communism. They will take over the government in The Hague and some minister will tell you to arrest all dissidents. And you will maintain order. You will send blue-uniformed constables armed with rubber truncheons and automatic pistols, helmeted perhaps, and carrying carbines. You'll have proper razzias with armored trucks blocking the street on each side. It's not unlikely you know. Just go outside and have a look at what's happening on the Newmarket Square right now."

"Who are you blaming?" the commissaris asked, tipping the ash of his cigar into the plastic skull.

"No one," Louis said quietly. "Not even the Germans, not even the Dutch police who took my grandparents away. Things happen, I told you already. I am not blaming things either, it's just that this idealizing, this reasoning, sickens me. If you want to do your job, if you consider your activity to be a job, do it, but don't ask me to clap my hands when you make your arrest. I don't care either way."

"It seems you are disproving your own theory," the commissaris said. "You refuse to do as you are told, don't you? You don't want to fit in. You should perhaps be finishing your studies so that you can join society on the right level, but you are working on the street market instead and driving a truck in some faraway country. But you are still doing something, working toward some goal. If you really believe what you say you believe, it seems to me you should be doing nothing at all. You should be drifting, pushed by circumstances of the moment."

"Exactly," Louis said. "That's what I am doing."

"No, no. You have some freedom, it seems to me, and you are using it. You are deliberately choosing."

"I try," Louis said, disarmed by the commissaris' quiet voice. "Perhaps you are right. Perhaps I am free in a way and trying to do something with my freedom. But I am not even very good at trying. I would never have done anything on my own. I was rotting away in a dark room, sleeping until two o'clock in the afternoon every day and hanging about in silly bars at night, when Abe found me. I just tagged on to Abe. It happened to me. He practically took me by the scruff of the neck and dragged me along."

"Didn't you say that you were making some structure out of beads? You were doing that before you met Abe, weren't you?"

"Yes, nothing ever came of it. I threw the whole mess into a dustbin one day. I had meant to create something really unusual, a human shape which would move in the wind or the draft. I was trying to make a body out of copper wire and connect the wire with thin plastic threads and string beads on the threads. The body would glitter and show life when it moved, but it wouldn't be moving itself, only acting when forces beyond its power played with it. Unfortunately I am no artist. The idea was good but I only managed to string a lot of beads together and waste a year."

"Right," Grijpstra said. "So Abe got you out of your mess. He may have got others out of their messes. But now he has been killed. The killer may want to kill other people like Abe."

"Rubbish."

"Pardon?"

"You heard me," Louis said sweetly. "Rubbish. Rot. Abe got killed because some force moved somebody's arm. The force was a haphazard force, like the wind. You can't catch the wind."

"If there's a draft we can find the crack and block it," the commissaris said.

"You can jail the instrument," Louis said stubbornly, "but you can't jail the force which activated the instrument. It's beyond you and the effort is silly. Why should I help you waste your time? You can waste it on your own."

"I see," the commissaris said, and looked at the trees again. There was no wind and the last rays of the sun were reflected in the small oblong mirrors of the young leaves.

"Do you really? You are an officer, aren't you? You direct the police?"

"I am a commissaris.* But if your theory is right I am only pretending to direct a shadow play which doesn't exist in reality. You are not original but you probably know you are not. Other people have thought of what you are thinking now. Plato, for instance, and others before him."

"There have been clever shadows on the planet," Louis said and smiled.

* The ranks of the Dutch municipal police are constable, constable first class, sergeant, adjutant, inspector, chief inspector, commissaris, chief constable.

"Yes. But you have helped us nevertheless. We know a little about the dead man now and we know a little about you. We are simple people, deluded probably, as you have pointed out already. We work on the assumption that the State is right and that public order has to be maintained.

"And we work with systems. Someone, some human who meant to harm Abe Rogge, has killed him. He had the opportunity to bash his face in and he thought he had a reason to do it. If we find somebody who had both the opportunity and the motive we will suspect him of a crime and we may arrest him. You, Louis Zilver, had the opportunity. You were in the house at the right time. But from what you have told us we may assume that you had no motive."

"If I was speaking the truth," Louis said.

"Yes. You have told us he was your friend, your savior in a way. He got you out of a rut. You used to spend your time lying in bed all morning and drinking all evening and trying to make a beady man all afternoon. You weren't happy. Abe made your life interesting."

"Yes. He saved me. But perhaps people don't want to be saved. Christ was a savior and they hammered nails through his hands and feet."

"A hammer," Grijpstra said. "I keep on thinking that Abe was killed with a hammer. But a hammer would have made a hole, wouldn't it? The face was bashed in over a large area."

"We'll find out what killed him," the commissaris said. "Go on, Mr. Zilver. You interest me. What else can you tell us?"

"Tell me," de Gier said, still holding Esther's hand, "why was your brother killed? Did he have any enemies?"

Esther had stopped crying and was caressing the table's surface with her free hand.

"Yes. He had enemies. People hated his guts. He was too successful, you see, and too indifferent. He was so full of life. People would worry and be depressed and nervous and he'd just laugh and go to Tunisia for a few weeks to play on the beach or to ride a camel to a little village somewhere. Or he would sail his boat onto the great lake. Or he would take off for the East and buy merchandise and sell it here and make a good profit. He was a dangerous man. He crushed people. Made them feel fools."

"Did he make you feel a fool?"

"I *am* a fool," Esther said.

"Why?"

"Everybody is. You are too, sergeant, whether you want to admit it or not."

"You were going to call me Rinus. O.K., I am a fool. Is that what you want me to say?"

"I don't want you to say anything. If you know you are a fool, Abe wouldn't have been able to hurt you. He used to arrange dinner parties but before anyone was allowed to eat anything, that person had to get up, face the assembled guests and say, "I am a fool.""

"Yes?" de Gier asked, surprised. "Whatever for?"

"He enjoyed doing things like that. They had to state that they were fools and then they had to explain why they were fools. Some sort of sensitivity training. A man would say 'Friends, I am a fool. I think I am important but I am not.' But that wouldn't be enough for Abe. He wouldn't let the man eat or drink before he had explained, in detail, why exactly he was a fool. He would have to admit that he was proud because he had some particular success, a business deal for instance, or an examination he had passed, or a woman he had made, and then he would have to explain that it was silly to be proud of such a feat because it had just happened to him. It wasn't his fault or merit, you see. Abe believed that we were just being pushed around by circumstances and that man is an inanimate mechanism, nothing more."

"And people had to admit it to him all the time?"

"Yes, that was the only way to start doing something."

"So they could *do* something after all?"

"Yes, not much. Something. Provided they admitted they were fools."

De Gier lit a cigarette and sat back. "Shit," he said softly.

"Pardon?"

"Never mind," de Gier said. "Your brother must have annoyed a lot of people. Did he ever admit he was a fool himself?"

"Oh, yes."

"And he really thought he was a fool?"

"Yes. He didn't care, you see. He just lived for the moment. A day consisted of a lot of moments to him. I don't think he cared when he died either."

"These friends he had, what sort of people were they? Business friends from the street market?"

Esther adjusted her hair and began to fiddle with the coffee machine. "More coffee, Rinus?"

"Please." She filled the apparatus and spilled some coffee on the floor.

"Allow me," de Gier said, and picked up a dustpan and a brush.

"Thanks. Are you married?"

"No, I live by myself, with my cat. I always clean up immediately when I make a mess."

"Friends, you said. Well, he often had friends from the street market in the house, and students would come, and some artists. And journalists, and girls. Abe attracted women. And Louis, of course, you have seen him in the corridor, haven't you. Where is he anyway?"

"He is upstairs with my colleague, Adjutant Grijpstra, and the commissaris."

"That little old man is your chief?"

"Yes. Can you describe some of his friends to me? I'll need a list of them. Did he have any special friends?"

"They were all special. He would get very involved with people, until he dropped them. He wasn't concerned about friendship, he always said. Friendship is a temporary phenomenon; it depends on circumstances and it starts and ends like the wind. He would annoy people by saying that, for they tried to attach themselves to him."

"Some case," de Gier said.

Esther smiled, a low tired smile.

"You remind me of the constables who came here a few days ago," she said. "They had the wrong number. Our neighbors had phoned. An old man was visiting them and the man suddenly got ill and collapsed. The neighbors had phoned for an ambulance but the police came as well, to see if there had been any violence, I suppose. The woman next door was very upset and I went there to see if I could be of some help. The old man was obviously dying. I think he had had a heart attack. I overheard the conversation between the constables."

"What did they say?" de Gier asked.

"The one constable said to the other, 'Hell, I hope the old bugger doesn't croak. If he does we'll have to write a report on it,' and the other one said, 'Never mind, he'll die in the ambulance and the health officers can take care of it.' "

"Yes," de Gier said.

"That's the way you people think, isn't it?"

"Not really," de Gier said patiently. "It's the way it sounds to you. You are involved, you see. The dead man is your brother. If a friend of mine dies, or if my cat gets run over, or if my mother gets sick, I'll be upset. I assure you that I will be very upset."

"But when you find my brother in a pool of blood . . ."

"I am upset too, but I keep the feeling down. I won't be of much help if I crack up, will I? And this looks like a strange case. I can't figure out why your brother was killed. Perhaps Grijpstra has seen something. You were here all afternoon, weren't you? Did anybody go up to his room?"

"No. Louis came in but I heard him pass the room and go up the second staircase to his own room."

"The Straight Tree Ditch is not a very busy thoroughfare," de Gier said, "but there must be people moving about in it. It would be possible to climb into the room from the street but it would be a real risk. Nobody has reported anything to the constables in the street, for they would have come in to tell me about it."

"Perhaps someone threw something at Abe," Esther said. "He could have been looking out at the canal. He often does. He stands at the window, the window is open, and he stares. He goes into a trance that way and I have to shout at him to break it. Somebody threw a stone at him perhaps."

"The stone would have fallen in the room or bounced off and got back to the street. The constables would have found it. A bloody stone in the street. I'll go and ask them."

He was back in a minute. "Nothing. I asked the men upstairs as well. There is a man from the fingerprint department. He says there is nothing in the room either. No weapon, no stone."

"Abe was a strange man and he died in a strange way," Esther said, "but there will be some technical explanation. There always is, for anything."

"Nothing is stolen, is there?"

"No. There is no money in the house, except what Abe keeps in his wallet. The wallet is still there, in the side pocket of his bush jacket. I saw the bulge. The pocket is buttoned. He usually has a few thousand guilders in it."

"That's a lot of money to keep in one's pocket."

"Abe always had money. He could make it much faster than he could spend it. He owns the warehouse next door; it's full of merchandise, and it never stays there long. There is cotton cloth in it now, bought just before the cotton price went up, and a whole floor stacked with cartons of wool, which he is selling in the street market."

"There is no connection between this house and the warehouse next door is there?"

"No."

"No secret door?"

"No, sergeant. The only way to get to the warehouse is via the street. The courtyards in the back are separated by a high brick wall, much too high to climb."

Grijpstra and the commissaris were coming down the stairs. De Gier called them in and introduced the commissaris to Esther. Two health officers were maneuvering their stretcher up the stairs, they had come with the Water Police launch.

"I'll go upstairs," de Gier said. "I think we would like to have the contents of the pockets before the body is taken away. You'll be given a receipt, Miss Rogge."

"Yes," the commissaris said. "We'll be off for a while now but we may have to come back later. I hope you don't mind the intrusion on your privacy, miss, but . . . ."

"Yes, commissaris," Esther said. "I'll be waiting for you."

The atmosphere in the street was still eerie. A siren wailed in the square nearby. A fresh platoon of riot police came marching up the narrow quay. Two launches of the Water Police, their foredecks packed with leather-coated constables ready to disembark, were navigating carefully between the moored houseboats and the launch preparing to take Abe Rogge's body aboard.

A young man, exhausted, was being run to the ground on the other side of the canal. Gloved hands grabbed his wrists and the detectives could hear the handcuffs' click and the man's sobbing breath.

"Where to, sir?" Grijpstra asked.

The commissaris was watching the arrest. "Hmm?"

"What now, sir?"

"Anywhere, a quiet place somewhere, a pub, a café. You go and find it. I am going back into the house a minute. When you find a good place you can telephone the Rogge house. The number will be in the book. Terrible, isn't it?"

"What, sir?"

"That manhunt just now. These riots bring out the worst in everyone."

"They weren't manhandling him, sir, they only made an arrest. The man has probably wounded a policeman in the square. They wouldn't go to so much trouble to catch him otherwise."

"I know, I know," the commissaris said, "but it's degrading. I have seen men hunted down like that during the war."

Grijpstra had seen it too but he didn't say anything.

"Right, run along."

"Sir," Grijpstra said and tapped de Gier on the shoulder.

"So where to?" de Gier asked. "Do you know anything here? The pubs will all be closed and I wouldn't want a police conference in a pub here right now anyway."

Grijpstra was staring at the policemen across the water. They were marching their prisoner to a Water Police launch. The prisoner wasn't resisting. Three men going for a walk.

"Hey."

"Yes," Grijpstra said. "The only place I can think of is Nellie's bar. It will be closed but she'll open up if she is in."

"Don't know the place."

"Of course you don't."

They read the sign together. It said, "If I don't answer the bell don't bang on the door for I won't be in." They read it three times.

"What nonsense," de Gier said finally. "If she isn't in she won't mind us banging on the door."

Grijpstra rang the bell. There was no answer. He banged on the door. A window opened on the second floor.

"Fuck off. Do you want a bucket of dishwater all over you?"

"Nellie," Grijpstra shouted, "it's me."

The window closed and they heard steps.

"It's you," Nellie said. "How nice. And a friend. Very nice. Come in."

The lights were switched on and they found themselves in a small bar. The only color in the bar seemed to be pink. Pink curtains, pink wallpaper, pink lampshades. Nellie was pink too, especially her breasts. De Gier stared at Nellie's breasts.

"You like them, darling?"

"Yes," de Gier said.

"Sit down and have a drink. If you buy me a bottle of champagne I'll give you topless service."

"How much is a bottle of champagne?"

"A hundred and seventy-five guilders."

"I am a policeman," de Gier said.

"I know you are, darling, but the police pay a hundred and seventy-five guilders too. I hate corruption."

"Do you ever have any policemen in here?"

Nellie smiled coyly and looked at Grijpstra.

"You?" de Gier asked.

"Sometimes," Grijpstra said, "but I don't pay. Nellie is an old friend."

"And you get topless service?"

"Of course he does," Nellie said briskly. "What will you have? It's a bit early but I'll mix you a cocktail. I don't serve straight drinks."

"No, Nellie," Grijpstra said. "We want to use your bar for an hour or so. Our commissaris wants a quiet place to talk; there will be some others as well. Do you mind?"

"Of course not, dear." Nellie smiled and bent over the bar and ruffled Grijpstra's hair. The breasts were very close to de Gier now and his hands twitched. "The bar is closed tonight anyway," Nellie crooned. "These damn riots are bad for business. I haven't seen a customer for two days and my runners can't get anyone through the roadblocks."

Her lips framed a snarl. "Not that I would welcome any customers these days, not with all this tension about."

"And you still dress like that?" de Gier asked, and stared.

Nellie giggled. "No. I wear jeans and a jersey, like

everybody else, but I don't want Grijpstra to see me in
a jersey. He is used to me like this, so I slipped on a
dress."

"Wow," de Gier said.

Nellie patted her breasts. "Disqualified me for a Miss
Holland contest once. I had too much, they said. But
they are good for business."

"Do you have a license for this place?" de Gier asked.
Her face clouded. "I thought you were a friend?"

"I am curious, that's all."

"No, I don't have a license. This isn't a real bar. It's
private. I only entertain one or two clients at a time.
The runners bring them in."

Prostitution, de Gier thought, straight prostitution.
He knew there were bars like Nellie's bar but he hadn't
come across one yet. Grijpstra had and he hadn't told
him. He looked at Grijpstra and Grijpstra grinned. De
Gier raised his eyebrows.

"Nellie had trouble once and I happened to answer
the call."

"That was a long time ago," Nellie said and pouted.
"You were still in uniform then. I haven't seen you for
a year; you are lucky I am still here." She groaned.
"That's the way it is. The nice ones are busy and they
don't pay and the bastards take far too much time, but
they pay."

De Gier could imagine what the bastards would be
like. The stray tourist, the lonely businessman. "Want a
nice woman, sir, something really special? Cozy place?
All to yourself? A little champagne? Not too expensive?
Let me show you the way, sir." And an hour, two hours
maybe, three hours at the most later, the bastard would
be in the street again with a stomach full of fuzz and a
light head and a light wallet. She would squeeze them
in stages. A pink spider in a pink web. And out the
minute they were dry, out into the street. And the run-
ner would be waiting and slip in for his cut and rush
out again, to catch the next fly.

"How's business, Nellie?"

She pulled in her underlip and bit it. "Not so good.

The guilder is too high and the dollar too low. I don't get them as I used to get them. It's Japanese now and they make me work."

A majestic woman, tall and wide-shouldered, with long red hair framing the green slanting eyes. De Gier could feel her strength. The strength of a voluptuous snake.

"Who is your friend, Grijpstra?"

"Sergeant de Gier," Grijpstra said.

"Nice. Very nice. I don't often see handsome men nowadays; they are getting scarce." The green eyes became innocent.

"Careful," Grijpstra said. "He has a way with ladies."

She giggled. "Don't worry, Grijpstra. I prefer your type, warm and heavy and fatherly. Handsome men make me nervous. They don't really need me and I hate it when I am not needed. Well, gentlemen, what can I do for you?"

"Let me use the phone," Grijpstra said.

She pushed the phone across the counter of the small bar and suddenly leaned over and kissed him full on the mouth. Grijpstra returned her kiss and reached out and patted her buttocks. De Gier looked away.

4

THE BELL RANG and de Gier went to open the door. The commissaris came in, followed by the doctor and the fingerprint man.

"Evening," the commissaris said brightly.

Grijpstra was rubbing his lips with a crumpled handkerchief. "Nellie's bar, sir, only place we could find. Very quiet."

"Your ears are red," de Gier said.

Grijpstra mumbled through his handkerchief. "Introduce me to the lady," the commissaris said, and climbed on a bar stool.

Nellie smiled and extended a hand. "A drink, commissaris?"

"A small jenever, if you have it."

Nellie poured six glasses.

"I thought you didn't serve straight drinks," de Gier said and looked at the woman's breasts again. He wasn't the only one who looked. The commissaris was fascinated; so was the doctor, so was the fingerprint man.

"Cleavage," the doctor said. "Lovely word, isn't it? Cleavage?"

The others grunted their agreement.

"Yes," the commissaris said and raised his glass, "but it isn't good manners to discuss a lady's anatomy in her presence. Cheers, Nellie."

The glasses were raised, emptied and plonked down on the counter. Nellie grabbed the bottle and filled them again.

"Lovely," the doctor said stubbornly. "As a doctor I should be immune perhaps but I am not. There is nothing more beautiful in the world. There are sunsets, of course, and sailing ships in a strong wind, and a deer running in a glade in the forest, and flowers growing on an old crumbling wall, and the flight of the blue heron, but nothing compares to the female chest. Nothing at all."

"Right," the fingerprint man said.

Nellie smiled and a slow ripple moved her bosom, a delicate ripple which started almost imperceptibly but gathered forced gradually and ebbed away again.

De Gier sighed. The commissaris turned his head and stared at de Gier.

"She charges a hundred and seventy-five guilders for a bottle of champagne," de Gier explained.

The commissaris inclined his small head.

"And then she takes off the top of her dress, sir, there's a zipper at the waist." De Gier pointed at the zipper.

Grijpstra had put his handkerchief away and was fumbling with a black cigar which he had found in a box on the counter. "What do you want the commissaris to do?" he asked gruffly. "Order champagne?"

The commissaris smiled and scraped a match. "Here," he said mildly. "It isn't the right night for champagne."

Grijpstra inhaled and glared at de Gier. The smoke burned Grijpstra's throat and he began to cough, pushing himself away from the bar and upsetting a stool. The smoke was still in his lungs and he couldn't breathe and he was stamping on the floor, making the glasses and bottles, lined up on narrow shelves attached to a large mirror, touch and tinkle.

"Easy," the doctor said, and began to pound Grijpstra's solid back. "Easy, put that cigar away!"

"No. I'll be all right."

"Syrup," Nellie said. "I have some syrup, dear."

The thick liquid filled a liqueur glass and Grijpstra swallowed obediently.

"All of it," Nellie said.

Grijpstra emptied the glass and began to cough again, the cigar smoldering in his hand.

"Stop coughing," de Gier said. "You have had your syrup. Stop it, I say." Grijpstra hiccupped. "That's better."

They drank their second glass of jenever and Grijpstra quieted down.

"We'll have to talk business," the commissaris said to Nellie. "I hope you don't mind, dear."

"Do you want me to go away?"

"Not unless you want to. Now, what did you think, doctor? You had time to study the body, did you?"

The doctor rested his eyes on the lowest point of Nellie's cleavage. "Yes," he said slowly. "Yes, quite. I had enough time although we'll have to do some standard tests later, of course. I have never seen anything like it. He must have been killed this afternoon, at four o'clock perhaps, or four thirty. The blood was fresh. I would think he was hit by a round object, small and round, like an old-fashioned bullet fired by a musket. But it looks as if he was hit several times. There were marks all over the face, or over the remains of the face, I should say. Every bone is smashed, jaws, cheekbones, forehead, nose. The nose is the worst. It seems that the object, whatever it was, hit the nose first and then bounced about."

"A musket," the commissaris said. "Hmm. Somebody could have stood on the roof of that old houseboat opposite the house and shot him from there. But it's unlikely. The Straight Tree Ditch has been patrolled

by riot police all afternoon. They would have noticed
something, wouldn't they?"

"Your problem, it seems," the doctor said. "All I
found was a corpse with a smashed face. Perhaps someone clobbered him with a hammer, jumped about like
a madman and kept on hitting him. How about that?"

He looked at the fingerprint man. The fingerprint man
was shaking his head.

"No?" the commissaris asked.

"Don't know," the fingerprint man said, "but I found
funny prints. There was blood on the windowsill, not
much, traces of blood really. But there was also blood
on the wall *above* the window, small imprints of a
round object, like the doctor said. Round. So the madman must have been banging away at the wall as well,
and on the windowsill. With a hammer with a round
head. There were imprints on the floorboards too."

"Sha," de Gier said.

"Pardon?" the commissaris asked.

"No," de Gier said, "not a hammer. But I don't
know what else."

"A ball," Grijpstra said. "A little ball which bounced
about. Elastic, a rubber ball."

"Studded with spikes," the fingerprint man said.
"That would explain the imprints. I photographed them
and we'll have them enlarged tomorrow. There were
marks, groups of red dots. Say you hammer a lot of
spikes into a rubber ball, the heads of the spikes will
protrude slightly. We can do a test. Leave some open
places so that the rubber can still touch whatever it hits
and bounce back."

"But there would have been a lot of balls, wouldn't
there?" the commissaris asked. "One ball wouldn't do
all that damage, so somebody would be pitching them
from the roof of that houseboat, one after another,
assuming Abe Rogge was standing in the window and
taking them all full in the face. And we found nothing.
Or did I miss anything?"

"No sir," Grijpstra said. "There were no balls in the room."

"Silly," de Gier said. "I don't believe a word of it. Balls ha! Somebody was there, right in the room, and hit him and went on hitting him. The first blow knocked him down and the killer couldn't stop himself. Must have been in a rage. Some weapon with spikes. A good-day."

"Yes," the commissaris said thoughtfully, "a good-day. A medieval weapon, a metal ball on the end of a short stick and the ball is spiked. Sometimes the ball was attached to the handle with a short chain. Would explain the marks on the wall and the windowsill, a weapon like that covers a sizable area. The killer swung it and he hit the wall with the backward stroke. What do you say, doctor?"

The doctor nodded.

"So the killer left and took the weapon with him. Nobody saw him, nobody heard him. The riots on the Newmarket may have drowned the noise."

"His sister heard nothing," de Gier said. "She was upstairs part of the time and in the kitchen part of the time. And that young fellow was upstairs too."

"Could have been one of them," Grijpstra said.

"They both benefit by the death," the commissaris said. "His sister inherits and the young man might believe he could take over the business. And we may assume that it was murder as there seems to have been some planning. The riots may have been used as cover and the weapon is unusual."

"Not necessarily," Grijpstra said. "There may have been a good-day on the wall, as a decoration. Someone lost his temper, grabbed it and . . ."

"Yes, yes," the commissaris said. "We'll have to find out, but I don't want to go back now. Tomorrow. You or de Gier, or both of you. There are a lot of suspects. These hawkers live outside the law. They don't pay much tax, sales tax or income tax. They always have more money than they can account for, put away in a tin or hidden in the mattress, or under a loose board. We may be dealing with armed robbery."

"Or a friend had a go at him," de Gier said. "His sister was telling me that he had a lot of arty friends. They would come for meals and drink and talk and he would play games with them, psychological games. They had to admit they were fools."

"What?" the commissaris asked.

De Gier explained.

"I see, I see, I see," the commissaris said, then smiled at Nellie.

"Another glass?" Nellie asked.

"No, coffee perhaps, or would that be too much trouble?"

"Coffee," Nellie said, "yes. It would be the first cup I ever served here. I can make some upstairs and bring it down."

The commissaris looked hopeful. "Does everybody want coffee?"

The five men agreed they all wanted coffee, eagerly, like small children asking for a treat. Nellie changed with them. Her smile was motherly, she wanted to care for them. The feeling in the pink whore's hole changed; the soft-shaded lights, the chintzy chairs, the two low tables with their plastic tops decorated with frilly doilies, the sickening disharmony of pinks, mauves and bloody and fleshy reds no longer inspired the urgency of sex but softened down into an unexpected intimacy; five male disciples adoring the goddess and the goddess cares and gives and flows and oozes and goes upstairs to make coffee in a percolator. Grijpstra reached across the bar and grabbed the stone jar of jenever. The glasses were refilled.

The commissaris sipped. "Yes," he said, and looked over his glass. "Strange place this. So all we have is questions. That remark of yours interested me, de Gier."

De Gier looked up, his thoughts had been far away. "Sir?"

"About Abe Rogge trying to make fools out of his friends. A powerful personality no doubt, even the

corpse looked powerful. So he humiliated his entourage.
The king and his court. One of the courtiers killed the
king."

"We only met one courtier," Grijpstra said, "that
young anarchist. Another strong personality."

"Intelligent young man," the commissaris agreed,
"and with a grudge. But a grudge against us, the police,
the State."

"Against power," Grijpstra said hesitantly.

"And Abe meant power to him?" the commissaris
asked. "No, I don't think so. It seemed to me he liked
Abe. Did that young lady you talked to like her brother,
de Gier?"

De Gier hadn't been listening. The commissaris repeated his question. "Oh yes, sir," de Gier said. "She
liked him, and they weren't in each other's way. They
lived separate lives, each on a separate floor. They only
had an occasional meal together."

"She wasn't dependent on him?"

"No, sir, she works for the university, has a degree."

"We might check her clothes for blood spatters."

"No, no," the commissaris said. "I saw her; she isn't
the type to jump about waving a good-day."

"That young fellow you were taking about?"

"No, not him either."

The fingerprint man shrugged.

The commissaris felt obliged to explain. "A man who
has killed another man an hour ago will be nervous.
Louis *was* nervous. The corpse, the crying sister, the
police tramping about. He was suffering from a slight
shock, but I didn't see any signs of a real mental crisis."

"You are the man who knows," the fingerprint man
said.

"No," the commissaris said, and drained his glass a
little too quickly. "I don't know anything. Whoever says
he knows is either a fool or a saint, a blithering fool or
a holy saint. But I have observed a number of killers
in my life. I don't think Louis has killed a man this
afternoon, but I could be wrong. In any case, he has
handled the corpse, he has been in the room. There'll

be some blood on his clothes, explainable blood, not enough to raise a serious suspicion. The judge won't be impressed."

Nellie came back with a full percolator and five mugs. They drank the coffee in silence.

"Thank you," the commissaris said, and wiped his mouth with his hand. "We'll go now. You have been very helpful, Nellie."

"Any time," Nellie said graciously, "but not when I have clients."

"We won't bother you. Grijpstra, would you mind asking about in the street? Perhaps the neighbors saw something. De Gier!"

"Sir."

"You come with me, I have another call to make tonight. I should take Grijpstra but you have more to learn."

They shook hands with Nellie and trooped out. De Gier was last.

"You are lovely," de Gier said quickly. "I would like to come back one evening."

"A hundred and seventy-five guilders," Nellie said, and her face looked cold and closed. "That'll be for the topless service, and the same for another bottle of champagne if you want more."

"Three hundred and fifty guilders?" de Gier whispered incredulously.

"Sure."

He closed the door behind him. The commissaris was waiting for him but at some distance. Grijpstra was closer.

"Did you try?" Grijpstra asked.

"Yes."

"Any luck?"

"Three hundred and fifty guilders."

Grijpstra whistled.

"What's the matter with the woman?" de Gier asked fiercely.

Grijpstra grinned.

"Well?"

"Her husband was a handsome man. Same size as you. Thick curly hair and an air force mustache. Could have been your brother. He invented that bar for her and lived off the spoils. Until he got knifed one night, by a Canadian sailor who wasn't used to jenever."

"De Gier," the commissaris called.

"Coming, sir," de Gier said.

5

THE SUDDEN TRANSITION shocked de Gier into consciously registering his surroundings. The small bar, in spite of its cheap gaudiness, had protected him somewhat and the lush femaleness of the hostess had lulled and excited him simultaneously, but now he was outside again, exposed to the clamor of shrieks and thuds and revving engines on the Newmarket and the plaintive wail of ambulances taking battered bodies to hospitals and racing back again. The clamor was far away, and half a mile of solid buildings, gable houses and warehouses and a few churches and towers shielded him from immediate violence, but the conflict's threat was all around him. His fear surprised him because he had never disliked violence before and he had certainly never run away from a fight, so why should he be glad to be out of it now? There would be plenty of opportunity on the square to practice his judo throws, to dodge attacks and have opponents floor themselves by their own weight and strength.

Perhaps it was the intangibility of the threat that unnerved him; the Straight Tree Ditch was quiet enough, guarded as it was by leather-jacketed riot police in pairs, strolling up and down, respectfully greeting the commissaris by either saluting or lifting their long truncheons. The elm trees were heavy and peaceful, their fresh foliage lit by street lights, and the ducks were asleep, floating about slowly, propelled by subconscious movements of their webbed feet, well out of the way of flying bricks, and the human shapes which had been diving into the cold dirty water to get away from charging constables and the relentless approach of police trucks and patrol cars—a common occurrence that night in the waterways closer to the Newmarket.

Grijpstra had marched away and the doctor and the fingerprint man were already on the launch. The commissaris, limping slightly, was a hundred yards ahead when de Gier finally shook himself free from his muddled thoughts. He sprinted and caught up with the commissaris, who looked approvingly at the sergeant.

"Nice," the commissaris said.

"What's nice, sir?"

"The way you sprint. If I run I get out of breath and the nerves in my legs play up." He looked at his watch. "Ten o'clock, we haven't wasted much time so far."

The commissaris turned into a narrow alley which led to another canal. They crossed a narrow footbridge. The commissaris was now walking briskly and his limp was less noticeable. De Gier ambled along, alert because they were getting closer to the Newmarket and might stumble into trouble, but the canal led nowhere, its water lapping gently at age-old crumbling quays and supporting more ducks, sleeping heaps of feathers emitting an occasional pleasant quack. De Gier remembered having read somewhere that ducks spend some twelve or more hours a day in a dream and he envied their daze, a condition preferable to human sleep on a bed. He was trying to imagine what it would be like to be a dazed duck, bobbing about in one of the city's many harbors or canals, when the commissaris stopped and pointed at a small houseboat.

"That's the one I was looking for," the commissaris whispered. "We are going in there and I want you to grab hold of yourself. A strange person lives on that boat but she is an old friend of mine and perhaps she will be of use. She may shock you perhaps but don't laugh or make a remark, never mind what she says or does. She won't be any good to us if we upset her."

"Yes, sir," de Gier whispered, awed by the unexpected warning. There was no need to whisper, the houseboat was still thirty feet away.

De Gier waited on the quay as the commissaris stepped on the short gangway, stood on the narrow ledge of the boat and knocked on the door. The houseboat looked pretty, freshly painted and its windows decorated with red and white checked curtains, tucked up in the middle and lifted toward the sides by pieces of laced braid, and framing geraniums in Delft blue china pots. Loving care had not been limited to the boat itself but had extended to the quay. A small garden grew on each side of the gangway, hemmed in by low ligustrum hedges and consisting of miniature rock gardens, the dislodged cobblestones piled up and serving as rocks, overgrown with trailers paying homage to the delicate orange labúrnum flowers which formed the centerpiece of the arrangement. The entire garden covered no more than some twelve square feet, but de Gier, a dedicated balcony gardener himself, was impressed and promised himself to find the spot again, perhaps just to stand there and gaze or perhaps to see if the designer's artfulness would inspire him to do something more imaginative with his flower boxes than he had been able to do so far.

"Who is it?" a heavy voice asked from within.

"It's me, Elizabeth," the commissaris shouted. "Me and a friend."

"Commissaris!" the voice shouted happily. "Come in! The door is open."

De Gier's eyes were round when he shook the lady's heavy hand. She was old, over seventy, he guessed, and dressed in a black gown which hung to the floor. There was a purse attached by straps to the leather belt which surrounded her ample belly, an embroidered purse with a solid silver handle. Gray hair touched her shoulders and there was a knitted cap on the large head.

"Sergeant de Gier," the commissaris said, "my assistant."

"Welcome, sergeant," Elizabeth said and giggled. "You are looking at my cap, I see. Looks funny, doesn't it? But there is a draft here and I don't want to catch another cold. I have had two already this year. Sit down, sit down. Shall I make coffee or would you prefer something a little stronger? I still have half a bottle of redberry jenever waiting for company but it may be too sweet for your taste. How nice to have visitors! I can't go for my evening walk with all this fuss on the Newmarket and I was just saying to Tabby here that there's nothing on TV tonight and he gets bored just sitting around with me, don't you, Tabby?"

Tabby sat on the floor, looking at de Gier from huge slit eyes, yellow and wicked. De Gier sat down on his haunches and scratched the cat behind the ears. Tabby immediately began to purr, imitating the sound of an outboard engine. He was twice the size of a normal cat and must have weighed between twenty-five and thirty pounds.

Elizabeth lowered her bulk into a rocking chair and pounded her thighs. "Here, Tabby." The cat turned and leaped in one movement, flopping down on his mistress's lap with a dull thud.

"There's a good cat," Elizabeth boomed, and squeezed the animal with both hands so that the air was forced out of its lungs in a full-throated yell, which made the commissaris and de Gier jump, but the cat closed its eyes with sensuous pleasure and continued its interrupted purring. "So? Berry jenever or coffee?"

"Coffee, I think, dear," the commissaris said.

"You make it, sergeant," Elizabeth said. "You'll find everything in the kitchen. I am sure you can make better coffee than I can, and while you are busy the commissaris and I can have a little chat. We haven't seen each other for months and months, have we, darling?"

De Gier busied himself in the kitchen, nearly dropping the heavy coffeepot as he thought of what he had just seen. When Elizabeth sat down he had glimpsed her feet, stuck into boots which would be size thirteen. De Gier had seen travesty before, but always in young people. Only a week ago he had helped to raid a brothel where the prostitutes were men and boys dressed up as females. When he had interrogated them, trying to find a suspect to fit the charge of robbery brought in by a hysterical client, he had been a little disgusted but not much. He knew that the human mind can twist itself into any direction. But de Gier had never met with an old man, an old big man, dressed up as a woman. Elizabeth was a man. Or was she? Was this a real case of a female mind accidentally thrown into the body of a male? The houseboat was definitely female. The small kitchen he was moving about in now showed all the signs of female hands having arranged its pots and pans, having sewed tableclothes and curtains to fit the cramped space, selected crockery in harmony with the neat array of cups on the top shelf of the cupboard and crocheted a small cloth in an attempt to make even the refrigerator look nice and dainty. The room where Elizabeth was now chatting to the commissaris—he could hear her deep voice coming through the thin partition—could be part of a Victorian museum; its armchairs, foot warmers, tea table, framed yellowish photographs of gentlemen with waxed mustaches and high collars had been high fashion, female fashion, a very long time ago.

"Can you manage, sergeant?"

De Gier shuddered. Elizabeth was in the open door, filling it completely; she had to bend her head.

"Yes, Elizabeth." His voice faltered. She was in the kitchen now and he could see the commissaris through the open door. The commissaris was gesticulating frantically. Yes, yes, he wouldn't give the game away, what *was* the silly little man worrying about?

"Yes, Elizabeth, the coffee is perking and I've got
sugar, cream, cups, spoons, yes, I've got it all."

"Naughty," Elizabeth said. "You haven't got the
saucers. You aren't married, are you, sergeant? Living
by yourself, I bet. You weren't planning to serve coffee
in cups only, were you? What do you think of these
cups? Bought them last week. Just what I've been
looking for for years. My mother had cups like that,
cost a few cents when I was a child and now you pay
as many guilders, but it doesn't matter, I bought them
anyway. And there's a saucer for Tabby too, nasty cat
goes on banging it about when I don't keep it filled;
he'll crack it if he isn't careful and I'll have to give him
an ugly enameled one again. Nasty cat, he got so angry
with me yesterday that he didn't watch where he was
going and he fell off the roof into the canal and I had
to fish him out with a broom and all I got for thanks
was a scratch. See here."

She rolled up her sleeve and de Gier saw a thick hairy
wrist with a deep scratch on it.

"I have a cat too," and he showed the top of his
right hand where Oliver had scratched him that morning.

"Ha," Elizabeth said, whacking him on the shoulder
so that he nearly dropped the sugarbowl, which he was
refilling from a tin found in the cupboard. "They all do
it, but what else can they do, the silly little animals!
They can't talk, can they? But they still have to show
their tempers. What's your cat? Alley cat or proper
aristocracy like my Tabby?"

"Siamese."

"Yes, they are nice too. I had one, years ago now.
The neighbor's dog got it when it was still small, grabbed
it by the neck and shook it and it was dead when he
dropped it. All over in a second. Since then I have
always had bigger cats. No dog would try to pick on
Tabby. He would be blind and castrated and floating in
the canal with his legs up if he only tried to look at my
Tabby."

She went back into the living room and de Gier

followed, carrying a tray. Elizabeth fussed with the cups
and brought out a tin with a Chinese design. "A biscuit,
gentlemen?"

De Gier was nibbling his biscuit, inwardly grumbling
about its oversweet taste when Elizabeth got up again
and opened a drawer. "Here, what do you think of it,
commissaris? Didn't I make a nice job of it? A hundred
and fifty hours of hard work, I timed it, but it was
worth the trouble, wasn't it?"

The commissaris and de Gier admired the bellpull
which Elizabeth dangled in front of their eyes. It showed
a repeating design of roses, embroidered in cross-stitch.
"I have lined it with the material you brought me in that
little plastic bag. They are clever nowadays, aren't they?
When I was a little girl you had to buy your material
by the yard, even when you only needed a little bit,
but now it's all supplied in those handy kits. Just the
right fit too. All I have to do now is find a set of copper
ornaments and sew them on and then I'll hang it over
there, next to the door. Just the right place for it. Maybe I'll get a brass bell as well and then I'll pull it and
the servant will come. Hahaha."

"Beautifully done, Elizabeth," the commissaris said.
"No, don't put it away, I want to see it properly. My
wife is doing something like that as well. On linen I
think she said it was, pure linen."

"Can't work on linen anymore," Elizabeth said sadly,
"not even with a magnifying glass. If the design isn't
printed on the cloth I can't follow it; on linen you have
to count the stitches, from a chart. I used to like doing
that but now I get a headache when I try. We are
getting old. It was very thoughtful of you giving me the
bellpull kit, commissaris. Good of you not to forget an
old woman living by herself."

"I like coming to see you," the commissaris said,
"and I would come more often if I wasn't so busy and
if my legs didn't make me ill all the time, but this visit
tonight isn't a social call. That's why the sergeant came
with me. He is a detective and we are working tonight.

There's been a manslaughter on the Straight Tree Ditch this afternoon."

"Manslaughter? Nothing to do with the riots, I suppose?"

"No. A man's face got bashed in. Abe Rogge, a hawker. The house is close, perhaps you know the man."

"That handsome man with the blond beard? Big fellow? With a golden necklace?"

"Yes."

"I know him." Elizabeth pursed her lips. "He has spoken to me. Often. He has even visited me here. He's got a stall on the Albert Cuyp street market in town, hasn't he?"

"Had."

"Yes, yes. Got killed, did he? What a shame. We haven't had any crime here for as long as I can remember. Not since those two idiot sailors clobbered each other years and years ago and I don't think they were ever charged. I pulled them apart and one of them slipped and fell into the canal."

She rubbed her hands gleefully. "Maybe I shoved him a little, did I? Hehehehe."

"Ah well, there has to be a first time for everything. Manslaughter, you said? Or murder? I saw some murders when I was on the force, but not too many of them, thank the Lord. Amsterdam isn't a murderous city although it's getting worse now. It's those new-fangled drugs, don't you think?"

"You were on the force?" de Gier asked in a sudden high voice. The commissaris kicked him viciously under the table and de Gier began to rub his shin.

"Constable, first class," Elizabeth said proudly, "but that was some years ago, before I retired. My health was a bit weak, you see. But I liked the job, better than being lady of the toilets. Five years on the force and thirty years in the toilets. I think I can remember most of my police days but there wasn't much happening when I was scrubbing floors and polishing taps and carrying towels and cakes of soap. And all these men pissing, piss piss piss all day. I thought in the end that that was all men ever do, hehehehehe."

The commissaris laughed and slapped his thighs and kicked de Gier under the table again. De Gier laughed too.

"I see," he said when he had finished laughing.

"But tell me about Abe Rogge's death, commissaris," Elizabeth said.

The commissaris talked for a long time and Elizabeth nodded and stirred her coffee and poured more coffee and handed out biscuits.

"Yes," she said in the end. "I see. And you want me to find out what I can find out. I see. I'll let you know. I can listen in the shops and I know a lot of people here. It's about time I paid some visits."

The commissaris gave her his card. "You can phone me in the evenings too. My home number is on the card."

"No," Elizabeth said. "I don't like telephoning gentlemen at their homes. The wives don't like it when a spinster like me suddenly wants to talk to hubby."

The commissaris smiled. "No, perhaps you are right. We'll have to be on our way, Elizabeth, thanks for the coffee, and you did a beautiful job on the bellpull."

"Commissaris," de Gier said when they were on the quay again.

"Yes?"

De Gier cleared his throat. "Was that really a friend of yours, commissaris?"

"Sure. I kicked you just in time, didn't I? I thought I had warned you before we went in. *That*, as you put it, once was Constable First Class Herbert Kalff. Served under me for a while, used to patrol this part of the city, but he had a problem as you will understand. He thought he was a woman and the idea got stronger and stronger. We put him on sick leave for a year and he was more or less all right when he came back but it started again. Claimed he was a girl and wanted to be called Elizabeth. He was on sick leave again and when there was no change we could only retire him. By that time she was a woman. There wasn't much medical science could do for her then. I imagine they operate on cases like that now. The poor soul has to live in a male body. She got a job as a lavatory lady in a factory but they made fun of her and she didn't last. She thinks that she was there for a long time but it isn't the truth. Her self-respect makes her say that. The truth is that she was declared unemployable and has lived on State money ever since. I've kept in touch and the social workers call on her but there was no need really; she has had a stable personality ever since she chose to be a woman, and she is incredibly healthy. She's over seventy, you know, and her mind is clear."

"Shouldn't she be in a home for the elderly?"

"No, the jokers would make fun of her. Old people are like children sometimes. We'll leave her here as long as possible."

"And you visit her regularly?" De Gier's voice was still unnaturally high.

"Of course. I like her. I like walking about this part of town and she makes a good cup of coffee."

"But he, she's mad!"

"Nonsense," the commissaris said gruffly. "Don't bandy that word about, de Gier."

They walked a while in silence.

"How's your rheuma, sir? You have been in bed for a while, they tell me."

"Incurable," the commissaris said pleasantly. "Drugs help a bit but not much. I don't like the medicines anyway. Horrible little pills, chemicals, that's all they are. Lying in a hot bath helps but who wants to be in a hot bath all day, like a frog in the tropics?"

"Yes," de Gier said, trying to think of a more helpful remark.

"And she isn't mad," the commissaris said.

"I can't understand it," de Gier said slowly. "The person is unnatural, absolutely, and you go to see her. Aren't you frightened or disgusted?"

"No. She is different, but that's all really. Some in-

valids look gruesome when you meet them for the first
time but you get used to their deformity, especially when
they are lovely people, just as Elizabeth is lovely. She
is a kind and intelligent person so why would you be
frightened of her? You are frightened of your own
dreams, it seems to me. You *do* dream, don't you?"

"Yes sir."

"Any nightmares?"

"Yes."

"What happens when you have a nightmare?"

"If it goes wrong I wake up in a sweat and I scream
but usually it doesn't come to that. I can control the
dreams somehow, get out of the most gruesome parts
anyway. I find a weapon in my hand and I kill whoever
is chasing me, or there's a car in the right spot and
I jump into it and they can't catch up with me."

"Very good," the commissaris said, and laughed.
"But you don't always get away, and then you suffer."

"Yes," de Gier said reluctantly.

"But why? The dream is part of you, isn't it? It's your
own mind. Why should your own mind frighten you?"

De Gier stopped. They had reached the narrow footbridge again and de Gier was ahead of the commissaris,
so the commissaris had to stop as well.

"But I can't avoid my dreams, can I, sir? I *can* avoid
that . . . well, apparition in the houseboat. It scares me.
I don't have to go there."

"Shouldn't I have taken you, sergeant?" the commissaris asked quietly.

"Well, yes, sir. Maybe it can help us with our investigation. It lives in the area and it has police training. May be useful. Yes, you should have taken me."

"So?"

"But you can't ask me to enjoy the experience."

"I am not aware that I am asking you to enjoy Elizabeth's company." The commissaris was smiling.

"No. Yes. Perhaps you are not. But you won't let
me . . ."

"Let you what?"

De Gier raised his hands helplessly and walked on,

slowly, so that the commissaris could keep up with him.

"We are all connected," the commissaris said softly. "Elizabeth is part of you, and you are part of her. Better face up to it."

They were passing the Rogges' house and Grijpstra was waiting at the door.

"Nothing, sir," Grijpstra reported. "The house on this side is a warehouse and it belongs to Abe Rogge. It's full of merchandise, wool and various types of cloth. Esther Rogge opened the door for me. Nothing there. The neighbors on the other side saw nothing special but they claim that quite a few people walked about this afternoon. The constables on duty let anybody through who lived here, without asking for any identification."

"Did you check the houseboat, Grijpstra?"

"Yes, sir. It's a wreck as you can see. Windows broken and everything. I found nothing extraordinary. A lot of rubbish, a broken fish knife and a plastic bucket and some rusted fishhooks and the usual collection of used condoms. I checked the roof as well but I had to be careful; the roof is rotten too, full of holes."

"Nobody fired a musket from there, you think? Or threw balls?"

"No, sir."

The launch had come back and was waiting for the commissaris. Grijpstra climbed aboard, de Gier hesitated.

"Don't you want to come, de Gier?" the commissaris asked.

"Perhaps I should have another talk with Esther Rogge and that young fellow, Louis Zilver. I would like to have a list of Abe's friends, and girlfriends."

"Can't it wait till tomorrow?"

"It could wait," de Gier said, "but we are here."

"Grijpstra?" Grijpstra looked noncommittal. "All

right," the commissaris said, "but don't overdo it. The woman is tired and that young man isn't very easy to get along with. Don't lose your temper."

"No, sir," de Gier said, and turned on his heels.

6

His suit was stained with soapstone powder and his right trouser leg smeared with red paint. He hadn't noticed anyone throwing paint but someone had. His socks were still wet, for although the water cannon hadn't hit him full on, he had been forced to run through puddles and mud had oozed into his shoes. He badly wanted to go home and have a hot shower and lounge about his small flat in the kimono he had bought at a department store where they were having a Japanese day. He wanted Oliver to be asleep on his legs while he looked through the paper and smoked and sipped tea. He also wanted a meal, some spaghetti perhaps, a dish he could cook quickly and tastefully, and Oliver would be sitting on the chair, his only chair, while he squatted on his bed and ate the spaghetti from a bowl. And then, afterwards, a cigarette on the balcony. He would have to do something about his flower boxes. He had lobelia in them again, and alyssum, like last year, and a geranium in a pot hanging from the wall. There might be more interesting plants. He stopped and

71

cursed. Elizabeth, the artful gardener. Nellie and her three hundred and fifty guilders. Had he joined the criminal investigation department to meet crazy people? To be with them? To try to understand them? To find, as the commissaris had suggested, his own connection with them? The commissaris! Silly little wizard with his limp?

"Mustn't talk about the commissaris like that, Rinus," he told himself. "You admire the man, remember? You like him. He is an advanced man, he knows far more than you do. He understands. He is on a different level. Higher, Rinus, much higher."

He stood at Esther's front door but he didn't ring the bell. The launch was taking off, the water sergeant was hauling in the mooring rope. The commissaris and Grijpstra were talking on the foredeck. They probably thought he had gone in already. He might not go in at all. What was he doing here anyway? Was he being the efficient policeman, efficient and energetic, going on when others were having a break? Or did he want to hold Esther's hand again?

A lovely woman, Esther. Not a cheap whore like Nellie who had bedazzled him with her big shapeful tits and low oozing voice, a gritty oozing voice. A voice can't be gritty and oozing at the same time but hers *was*. It *was*, damn it. "Easy, Rinus," he told himself. "You are losing control. Today has been too much for you. A battered corpse and a whole square full of dancing idiots throwing soapstone powder and paint and all those uniformed bullies charging the idiots and the sirens, it was too much for you. The commissaris shouldn't have left you, he knew you were cracking up. But he left you all the same, didn't he?"

De Gier listened to the silence of the canal. So he had. And if the commissaris had left him on his own he must have had faith. Policemen don't usually work on their own, they work in pairs. Detectives work in pairs too. So that the one can check the other, restrain him if necessary if he loses his temper, or touches his gun. The one policeman protects the other by restraining him. He protects him against himself. It is the task of the police to protect the civilian against himself. It is the task of the policeman to protect his mate against himself. He was talking aloud now, droning the words.

"Shit," de Gier said and pressed the bell.

Esther opened the door.

"You," Esther said. "Sergeant Rinus de Gier."

De Gier tried to smile.

"Come in, sergeant."

Esther looked better. There was color on her face again and she had made up her lips.

"I am having something to eat. Would you care to join me, sergeant?"

"Please."

She led the way to the kitchen. He was given a plate of soup, hot tomato soup from a tin. De Gier didn't like tomato soup and never ate the bloody-looking fluid but he didn't mind now. She cut him a piece of bread and there were gherkins on the table and olives, and a piece of blue-veined cheese. He ate it all while Esther watched him.

"We can have coffee upstairs."

He hadn't said anything during the meal and now he merely nodded.

"A nice room," de Gier said, from the deep low chair Esther had directed him to, "and you have a lot of books."

Esther waved at the two walls covered by bookcases. "A thousand books and I have learned nothing from them. The piano has been of more use to me."

He got up and walked toward the baby grand. An etude by Chopin was lying on the stand and he put a hand on the keyboard and picked away, trying to read the notes.

"That's very nice," Esther said. "Do you play often?"

"No. I had piano lessons as a child but I switched to the flute. I play with Grijpstra, the adjutant you met today."

"What does he play?"

"Drums," he said and grinned. "Someone left a set of drums in our office at Headquarters, years ago now, we have forgotten why, but Grijpstra remembered that he played drums once and started again and I found my flute. It's a silly combination perhaps but we manage."

"But that's beautiful," Esther said. "Why shouldn't drums and flute go together. I'd love to hear you play. I could play with you too. Why don't you both come one evening and we can try?"

"It's free music," he said. "We have some themes we use, church music mostly, sixteenth and seventeenth century, but then we go off and we play anything. Trills and bangs."

"I'll fit in somehow," Esther said confidently.

He laughed. "O.K. I'll ask Grijpstra."

"What else do you do?" Esther asked.

"I fuss with my cat and I try to do my job. Like tonight. I've come to ask you questions. If you don't mind, of course. I'll come back tomorrow if you mind."

She sat down on the piano stool. "Right, sergeant, go ahead. I feel better now, better than I did this afternoon. I have even slept for an hour. Maybe one shouldn't sleep when one's brother has been murdered, but it seemed the best thing to do. He was my last relative, I am alone now. We are Jewish. Jews think that families are very important; perhaps we are wrong. People are alone, it's better to realize the truth. I never had much contact with Abe, no real contact. You are alone, too, aren't you?"

"Yes."

"You understand perhaps."

"Perhaps. Did your brother have a weapon in his room, a funny weapon? Something with a studded ball at its end, a weapon which can be swung?"

"A good-day?" Esther asked. "You mean that medieval weapon? I know what it is. It is often described in Dutch literature and in history. I took history at university, Dutch history, murder and manslaughter through the ages. Nothing changes."

"Yes, a good-day."

"No, there was no weapon in Abe's room. He used to carry a gun, a Luger I think it was, but he threw it into the canal years ago. He said it no longer fitted his philosophy."

Esther fumbled in her handbag. "Here, I found this, his passport and a notebook."

He looked through the passport and saw visas for Czechoslovakia, Rumania and Poland. There were also entry and exit stamps from Tunisia and Morocco. The notebook contained names and telephone numbers.

"A hundred names," he said. "Too many to investigate. Any close friends? Boyfriends? Girlfriends?"

"Girls," Esther said. "Just girls. Lots and lots and lots. Two a day sometimes, more even. It disgusted me to see them trooping in and out. Last Sunday he had three, just after he had come back from Morocco. They couldn't wait. He had one before each meal. The first came before breakfast. She is a tourist guide and starts early but she had to have her sex first."

De Gier wanted to whistle but rubbed his chin instead. "And he accommodated them all?"

"The pretty ones."

"Were all his contacts as casual as that?"

"No. He would go and see Corin. She works at the university with me. I don't think he just slept with her although perhaps he did. Corin never discussed him much. Her name is in the notebook, I'll mark it. Corin Kops. You can find her address in the telephone directory."

"Anyone else?"

"Yes, a student, a very young girl. Studies medicine. I think he was fascinated by her or perhaps she just annoyed him. Wouldn't give in so easily. I'll mark her name as well. Tilda van Andringa de Kempenaar."

"Beautiful name."

"Yes, she is nobility, perhaps that's why she won't give in. Blue blood."

"Copulation doesn't mean an introduction," de Gier said, and grinned. His sanity had returned, or rather, it

was beginning to return. He still felt shaken. He closed
his eyes and tried to think.

"You aren't falling asleep, are you?" Esther asked.
"You must be very tired. Shall I give you a blanket?
You can sleep on the couch if you like. I'll wake you
up at any time you say."

"No, no, I have to go home to feed my cat. Thanks
anyway. Business, that's what I wanted to ask. Do you
have his business records here? I'd like to look through
them. I am no expert at bookkeeping but I'd like to
have some idea about the size of his transactions."

"Louis takes care of his books, he's got them upstairs. He is in now. I'll ask him if you like."

De Gier had been hearing an irregular buzzing sound
for the last ten minutes and a noise which seemed like
scraping. It came from the floor above and he looked
at the ceiling.

"Is *he* making that noise upstairs?"

She giggled. "No, maybe the killer has returned and
is whirring his deadly ball. Why don't you go up and
have a look?"

He didn't feel like leaving the comfortable chair but
he got up obediently.

"Yes," Louis said, and looked up at de Gier who had
opened the door. He was sitting on the floor and picked
up a toy mouse, winding its clockwork. De Gier's mouth
was half open. He hadn't expected what he saw. The
floor was full of small tin animals—mice, birds, turtles,
frogs, even moles and giant beetles. Most of them were
moving. The mice stood up every two seconds and then
fell down again, busily going on with their zigzag tours
on the bare boards of the floor. The frogs jumped, the
turtles ambled, the birds hopped and waved their tails,
the beetles zoomed. Every now and then one of them
would stop, and Louis would pick it up and wind the
key. Some of them had pushed themselves against the
wall and were burring aimlessly. A bird had been
stopped by a small carpet and was jumping feebly, try-

ing to pass the obstacle. A beetle had fallen on its side and its motor was whirring at full speed.

"Samples," Louis said loudly. "Abe bought a few thousand of them and I took these from the warehouse. Most of them work. Crazy, isn't it?"

"Yes," de Gier said. "How long have you been playing with them?"

"Only started just now. It's amusing isn't it? I had them when I was a child but never more than one at a time. Businessmen can amuse themselves on a large scale as you see. No child will ever have a collection like this."

De Gier had squatted down and saved the animals who had got stuck at the wall, by pointing them at the center of the room. "Hey," Louis said. "I didn't invite you to join me, did I?"

"No," de Gier said, and wound up a frog.

"Never mind. You can play if you like. Have the police made any progress in the case yet?"

"No. The police are baffled."

"It's human fate to be baffled," Louis said, and began to sweep up the toys, wrapping each animal in tissue paper, and replacing it in a carton.

"I hear you kept Abe Rogge's books. Can I see them?"

Louis pointed at the desk. "It's all there, you can take them with you if you like. I have kept the books up to date, the accounting is simple. Most purchases are covered by invoices and they are all paid. Our sales were mostly for cash and they are entered in a cash book. And there's some wages-administration; only Abe and myself are on the payroll."

"Your warehouse is full of goods, I hear."

"Yes."

"All paid for."

"Yes."

"How much do you have in stock?"

"In money?"

"Yes."

"A hundred and twenty thousand guilders and something."

"That's a lot," de Gier said, "and all paid for. Was Abe financing his own deals?"

Louis laughed. "The bank wouldn't give us a penny, they don't back hawkers. Abe borrowed from friends. Mostly from Bezuur, his oldest and best friend."

"So he had friends," de Gier said and nodded. "Very good."

Louis looked up from his packing. "The police would suspect friends, wouldn't they? Friends are close and friendship can change into hatred. Two sides of the same coin."

"Yes, yes. Who is Bezuur?"

"A rich man, a very rich man. He and Abe went to school together, to school and to the university. They both dropped out. They studied French. They also traveled together, mostly in France, of course, and in French North Africa. They also traded together but Bezuur's father died and left him a big business, earth-moving equipment. He's a millionaire."

"And he lent Abe money?"

"Yes, at bank interest. Eleven percent we are paying now. The firm owes him sixty thousand, to be repaid in three months' time when we have moved the stocks in the warehouse, maybe earlier. Abe was planning a long holiday and I was supposed to go with him."

"North Africa again?"

"No, we planned to sail a boat to the Caribbean."

"And what happens now?"

"I'll sell the stocks. I phoned Bezuur about an hour ago to tell him about Abe's death. He said I can go on with the business if Esther lets me, for she will inherit it. And I can repay the loan as planned."

"Did you speak to Esther?"

"Not yet."

"And what will you do when you have moved the stocks?"

"No idea. Find a partner maybe and go on as before. I like this business, especially the irregularity of it."

"And if Esther won't let you go on?"

Louis shrugged and smiled. "I don't care. Bezuur will sell the stocks and get his money back and the rest will go to Esther. I'll just leave. Nobody depends on me."

"Detached, are you?" de Gier said, offering a cigarette.

"Thanks. Yes. I am detached. To hell with it. But I am sorry Abe died, I enjoyed being with him. He taught me a lot. If he hadn't taught me I would be very upset now but you find me playing happily with clockwork animals. And I am not pretending. Any more questions?"

"Was Abe close to anyone else? Any enemies? Competitors?"

Louis thought, taking his time. "He slept with a lot of girls," he said in the end. "Perhaps he stepped on somebody's toes. I am sure some of those girls had lovers, or husbands even. He behaved like a stud bull at times. And he insulted people, of course. Insulted them by not caring. They could go blue in the face and blow steam out of their ears and he would just laugh, not offensively to annoy them, but because he didn't care. He would tell them they were balloons, or stuffed lifeless animals."

"But he included himself, didn't he?"

"Oh yes, he refused to see any value anywhere."

"So why did he make money then?"

Louis got up and put the carton in a corner of the room. "If nothing matters you can laugh and you can cry, can't you?" De Gier looked blank. "Abe preferred to laugh, with a full belly and a cigar in his mouth and a car parked in the street and a boat in the canal. I don't think he would have minded if he hadn't had any of those things, but he preferred having them."

"Ah yes," de Gier said.

"You don't understand," Louis said. "Never mind."

"You really admired him, didn't you?" de Gier asked viciously.

"Yes, copper, I did. But now he is dead. The balloon has burst. More questions?"

"No."

"Then I'll go to the nearest pub and have six glasses of colored alcohol, and then I'll go and sleep somewhere. There'll be a girl in the pub who'll let me go home with her. I don't want to spend the night here."

De Gier got up from the floor and left the room. He was too tired to think of any suitable repartee. He found the toilet before he returned to Esther's room and washed his face with cold water. There was a small mirror in the lavatory and he saw his own face. His hair was caked with soapstone powder and mud and there were paint spatters on his cheeks; the eyes looked lifeless, even his mustache drooped.

"Well?" Esther asked.

"I heard the name Bezuur."

"Klaas Bezuur," Esther said slowly, inviting him with a gesture to sit in the easy chair again. "Yes, I should have mentioned him but I haven't seen Klaas for such a long time that I have forgotten him. He asked me to marry him once but I don't think he meant it. Abe and he were very close once, but not anymore."

"Did they fall out?"

"No. Klaas became rich and he had to give up working in the street market and traveling about with Abe. He had to take care of his business. He lives in a villa now, in one of the new suburbs, Buitenveldert I think."

"I live in Buitenveldert," de Gier said.

"Are you rich?"

"No, I have a small flat. I expect Bezuur lives in a quarter-of-a-million bungalow."

"That's right. I haven't been to the house although he has asked us but Abe didn't want to go. He never visited anyone unless he had a good reason, sex, or a party, or a business deal, or a book he wanted to discuss. Klaas doesn't read. He's a bit of a slob now; he was very fat and closed up the last time I saw him."

"I'd better go," de Gier said, rubbing his face. "Tomorrow is another day. I can hardly see straight."

She saw him to the door. He said good night and meant to walk away but stopped and stared at the canal's surface. A rat, frightened by the tall looming shape of the detective, left its hiding place and jumped. The sleek body pierced the oily surface with a small splash and de Gier watched the converging circles fading out slowly.

"Aren't you going?" a voice asked, and he looked around. Esther stood at the open window of her room on the second floor.

"Yes," he called back softly, "but don't stand there."

"He can throw his ball," Esther said, "if he wants to. I don't mind."

De Gier didn't move.

"Rinus de Gier," Esther said, "if you aren't going you may as well come in again. We can keep each other company." Her voice was calm.

The automatic lock clicked and de Gier climbed the two flights of stairs again. She stood at the window when he came in, and he stood behind her and touched her shoulder. "The killer is a madman," he said softly. "To stand here is to invite him."

She didn't reply.

"You are alone in the house. Louis told me he is sleeping out. If you like, I'll telephone Headquarters and we'll have two constables guarding the house. The riot police have gone."

"Here," he said and gave her the toy mouse he had put in his pocket when Louis wasn't looking. Esther had left the window and was wandering through the room. She was looking at the tin animal as if she didn't know what it was.

"A mouse," de Gier said. "You can wind it up and put it on the floor. It walks and it jumps a bit. It's yours."

She laughed. "What's this? Shock treatment? I didn't

know the police had become subtle. Are you trying to unnerve me so that I'll drop my defense and give you a valuable clue?"

"No," de Gier said. "It's a clockwork mouse."

"Abe used to give me things too. Seashells and bits of driftwood and dried plants. He would buy them on the market or find them on the beach somewhere and keep them in his room, and then he would suddenly come into my room, usually when he thought that I was depressed about something or other, and give me a present. I still have some of them."

She pointed at a shelf and de Gier saw some shells, bits of white and pink coral, a twig with dried seedpods.

Esther was crying. "A drink," she said. "We need a drink. He has a bottle of cold jenever in the fridge, I'll go and get it."

"No, Esther. I have to go, but you can't stay here by yourself."

"Do you want me to come home with you?"

De Gier scratched his bottom.

She giggled through her tears. "You are scratching your bottom, are you nervous? Don't you want me to come home with you? I'll go to the police hotel if you have one, or you can lock me in a cell for the night."

De Gier adjusted his scarf and buttoned his jacket.

"You look a bit scruffy," Esther said, "but you have had a hard day. You are still handsome. I'll come home with you if you like. The house makes me nervous. I keep on thinking of Abe's face and that spiked ball you all keep talking about. A good-day you said. It's all too horrible."

De Gier brushed his mustache with his thumb and index finger. The hairs were sticking together, he would have to wash it. He grimaced. He would get soap in his mouth. He always got soap in his mouth when he washed his mustache.

"You aren't a sexual maniac, are you?" Esther asked. "It'll be safe to go home with you?" She laughed. "Never mind. If you are a maniac you'll be a very tired maniac. I'll probably be able to handle you."

"Sure," de Gier said. "Why were you standing at the window?"

"I heard a splash. I thought the killer had come back and that he had dropped his ball into the canal."

"So why go to the window? It's the most dangerous place in the house. Abe got killed at the window, or, rather, we think so now."

"I don't mind."

"You want to die?"

"Why not?"

"You are alive," de Gier said. "You'll die anyway. Why not wait?"

Esther stared at him. He noticed that she had a thick underlip and a wide nicely curved upper lip.

"All right," de Gier said. "I'll take you to my sister's place or anywhere else you want to go. You must have friends in town. This Corin lady you mentioned just now, for instance. Or relatives. Or I can take you to a hotel; there are lots of hotels. I have a car, it's parked near the Newmarket. I'll go and pick it up and you can pack a bag. I'll be back in five minutes."

"I'll go with you and come back tomorrow. Perhaps it'll be better tomorrow. I have washed the floor of Abe's room. I won't stay here tonight."

"I have a cat," de Gier said as he opened the door of the car for her. "He's very jealous. He'll probably want to scratch you and he'll wait for you in the corridor in case you want to go to the toilet. Then he'll jump you suddenly and yowl. He may also piss on your clothes."

"Maybe I should go to a hotel after all."

"If you want to."

"No," she said and laughed. "I don't mind your cat. I'll be nice to him and my clothes will be in my bag. It's a plastic bag and it's got a zip. I'll pick him up and turn him over and cuddle him. Cats like to be cuddled."

"He can't stand it if people are nice to him," de Gier said. "He won't know what to do."

"There'll be two of us," Esther said.

De Gier was on the floor, trying to adjust to the hardness of his camping mattress. Esther was standing in the open door of his small bedroom, her finger on the light switch.

"Good night," Esther said.

"Good night."

"Thanks for the use of your shower."

"You are welcome."

"Your bed looks very comfortable."

"It's an antique," de Gier said from the floor. "I found it at an auction. The man said it came from a hospital."

"I like the frame," Esther said. "All those ornate metal flowers. And it's very nicely painted. Did you do it yourself?"

"Yes. It was a hell of a job. I had to use a very fine brush."

"I am glad you didn't use a lot of colors. Just gold, lovely. I hate these new fads. Some of my friends have used all the colors of the rainbow to decorate their houses, and those horrible transfers! Butterflies in the toilet and animals on the bath and funny pictures in the kitchen and you are forced to read the same jokes over and over again. Bah!"

"Bah!" de Gier said.

"This must be a good place to live in. Just a bed and a bookcase and a lot of cushions and plants. Very good taste. Why do you have the one chair? It doesn't seem to fit in."

"It's Oliver's. He likes to sit on a chair and watch me eat. I sit on the bed."

She smiled.

Beautiful, de Gier thought, she is beautiful. She had turned the switch now and the only light in the room came from a lantern in the park. He could only just make out her shape but the light caught the white of her

breasts and face. She was wearing his kimono but she
hadn't tightened the sash.

She can't feel like it now, de Gier thought. Her
brother died today. She must still be in a state of shock.
He closed his eyes, trying to destroy the image in his
bedroom door but he could still see her. When she
kissed him he groaned.

"What's wrong?" she asked softly.

He groaned again. The commissaris will find out.
Grijpstra will find out. And Cardozo, the new detective
on the murder squad, will find out and make sly re-
marks. And Geurts and Sietsema will know. The murder squad will have something to discuss again. De Gier
the ladykiller. A detective who goes to bed with suspects. But he hadn't planned it. It had happened. Why
will they never accept that things happen? Oliver yowled
and Esther jumped.

"He bit me! Your cat bit me! He sneaked up to me
from behind and bit me! Ouch! Look at my ankle!"

The light was on again and de Gier rushed to the
bathroom and came back with a bandage. Oliver sat
on the chair and watched the scene. He looked pleased.
His ears pointed straight up and his eyes looked bright.
His tail flicked nervously. Esther tickled the cat behind
the ears and kissed him on the forehead. "Silly cat,
aren't you? Jealous cat! It's all right, I won't take him
away from you."

Oliver purred.

She switched the light off and took de Gier by the
hand.

The kimono had dropped to the floor. Oliver sighed
and curled up.

"He doesn't watch, does he?" Esther whispered on
the bed.

De Gier got up and closed the door.

7

"No, DEAR," the commissaris' wife said sleepily, and turned over. "It's still early, it's Sunday. I'll make the coffee a little later, let me sleep awhile, sleep sleep . . ."

The rest of the sentence was a mumble, a mumble which changed into a soft pleasant polite snore. The commissaris patted her shoulder with a thin white hand. He hadn't asked for coffee, he hadn't said anything at all. She had probably noticed that he was awake and her sense of duty had been aroused. Dear Katrien, the commissaris thought, dear excellent soul, soul of souls, you are getting old and weak and tired and there are more lines in your face than I can count. Have you ever shared my thoughts? Perhaps you have.

He patted her shoulder again and the gentle snore changed into deep breathing. He sat up and pushed the blankets away and crossed his legs, straightening his spine. He lit a small cigar and inhaled the first smoke of the day, blowing it away toward the open window. In the garden his turtle would be rowing about in the grass. It was eight o'clock and Sunday morning. The

city was silent without the growl and clank of traffic.
A thrush sang in the garden, the sparrows had left their
nests above the drainpipe and were rummaging about in
the hedge, twittering softly, and the magpies were looking for more twigs to reinforce their domed nest in the
poplar. He could hear the flap of their wings as they
wheeled about just outside his window. He grunted con-
tentedly.

There had been a dream and he was searching for its
memory. It had been an interesting dream and he
wanted to experience it again. Something to do with the
garden, and with the small fishpond at the foot of the
poplar, and with a splash. He sucked his cigar and the
dream came back to him. He had been in the garden
but his garden had been much bigger, spreading far
into the distance, and the fishpond had been a vast lake.
And the poplar was a forest, and the turtle was close.
The turtle was his ordinary size, small, compact, self-
contained and friendly, with a lettuce leaf in his mouth.
The commissaris had been expecting something and so
had the turtle, for it was craning its leathery neck and
chewing excitedly. It had been staring at the blue
metallic sky and the round white moon flooding the
lawn with soft downy pale light.

And then it came. A purple spot growing quickly in
size. Mauve and moving. Splitting into two individual
but similar shapes. Female, with large wings. They were
so close that he could see their long limbs, curved
breasts, calm faces. He saw their features, high cheek-
bones and slanting eyes. Quiet faces but intent, purpose-
ful. Wings fluttered as they turned above him, him and
the turtle, who had lost his benign solitude and was
trying to dance in the high grass and had dropped his
lettuce leaf. The commissaris was squatting down, holding on to the turtle's shield. He recognized the winged
shapes' faces. They resembled the Papuan who had
once been arrested by the murder-squad detectives and
who had escaped again without leaving a trace. Perhaps they were his sisters. Or his messengers. Or his
thoughts, reaching out from wherever he was now. The

commissaris lost his association. The apparitions were so close above him now that he could have touched their slender ankles if he had reached out. The wings moved again and they were gaining height. They hovered above the lake and then, first one, then the other, folded their wings, and dropped. They hit the surface of the lake like arrows and plunged right through.

The turtle had lost all self-control and was capering about at the commissaris' feet, distracting his attention. When he looked up again the mauve figures were with him on the grass, with spread wings, observing him and showing a glimmer of amusement in their sparkling eyes and softly smiling mouths. That was the dream. He rubbed the bald spot on his skull, amazed that the dream had come back to him. He didn't like purple or mauve and he had never been particularly impressed by naked winged angels. Where had the images come from? He now also remembered the events of the previous evening. Nellie's bar. Nellie's colors had been purple and mauve too, and pink, of course. He saw Nellie's large solid breasts again and the cleavage the doctor had been so poetic about. Had Nellie so impressed him that she had helped form this dream, together with the sympathetic presence of his turtle and the glorified version of his garden and the Papuan, a man he had liked once and whose attitude had puzzled him at the time?

The commissaris sighed. It had been a good dream. He picked up the phone and dialed a number. The phone rang for a long while.

"De Gier." The voice on the phone sounded deep and throaty.

"Morning, de Gier."

"Sir. Good morning, sir."

"Listen," the commissaris said. "It's early and it's Sunday, and judging from the way you talk you were asleep when your phone rang, I want you to get up and wash and have some coffee and shave perhaps. When you are ready you can phone me back. I'll be waiting for you."

"Yes, sir. Ten minutes."

"Make it twenty. You can have breakfast first if you like."

"Right," de Gier said.

The commissaris replaced the phone and stretched out. Then he changed his mind and got up and fetched some lettuce leaves from the kitchen. The turtle was waiting for him in the garden and bravely left the grass and marched ponderously on the flagstones leading to the open door of the commissaris' study.

"Morning sir," de Gier said again.

"Tell me," the commissaris said, "about last night. Anything worthwhile?"

"Yes," de Gier said. "Miss Rogge gave me three names and three addresses. Do you have a pen, sir?"

The commissaris noted the names and addresses. De Gier talked. "Yes, yes, yes," the commissaris said.

"Perhaps Grijpstra and I should call on these people today, sir."

"No. Grijpstra can go and I'll go with him. I have other plans for you. Are you ready?"

"Yes, sir."

"Right. Go to our garage and ask for the gray van. Then go to the stores. We have some confiscated textiles, bales of cloth, a good assortment. They are due for auction next week but we can have them. I'll phone the chief clerk at his home later this morning."

"Textiles?" de Gier asked. "The gray van? Do you want me to take the textiles somewhere?"

"Yes. To the street market tomorrow. A detective should be a good actor; tomorrow you can be a hawker. I'll contact the market master at the Albert Cuyp and he'll give you a stall and a temporary license. You won't need more than a few days. Make friends with the other hawkers. If the killer comes from the market you'll be able to pick up a trail."

"Just me, sir?" De Gier didn't sound pleased.

"No. You can take Sergeant Sietsema with you."

"Can't I have Cardozo?"

"Cardozo?" the commissaris asked. "I thought you didn't like Cardozo. You two are always quarreling."

"Quarreling, sir? We never quarrel. I have been teaching him."

"Teaching. O.K. Take him. Perhaps he's the right choice. Cardozo is Jewish and Jews are supposed to be good traders. Maybe he should be the hawker and you can be his assistant."

"I'll be the hawker, sir."

The commissaris smiled. "Right. Phone Cardozo and get him to join you today. Better phone him right now before he leaves for the day. And what about Esther Rogge, was she in a good state of mind when you left her last night?"

There was no answer.

"De Gier?"

"I have her here with me, sir, in my apartment."

The commissaris looked out of the window. One of the magpies was sitting on the grass, looking at the turtle. The turtle was looking back. He wondered what the two could have in common.

"It isn't what you are thinking, sir."

"I wasn't thinking, de Gier, I was looking at my turtle. I had a dream last night, something to do with the Papuan. Do you remember the Papuan?"

"Yes, sir."

"A strange dream. Something about his two sisters. They had wings and they flew into my garden. There was a full moon and my turtle was in the dream as well. My turtle was excited, jumping about in the grass."

"In your dream, sir?"

"Yes. And it was real, more real than the conversation I am having with you now. You dream too, you told me last night."

"Yes, sir. I'd like to hear more about your dream sometime."

"Sometime," the commissaris said, and stirred the coffee which his wife had put on the little table next to his bed. "Sometime we'll talk about it. I often think about the Papuan, possibly because he was the only

suspect who ever got away after we had caught up with
him. You'd better get Miss Rogge home, I suppose.
I'll phone you tonight and tell you what Grijpstra and
I found out, or you can phone me. My wife will know
where I am."

"Sir," de Gier said, and rang off.

By eleven o'clock the commissaris' black Citroën was
parked outside Grijpstra's house on the Lijnbaansgracht
opposite Police Headquarters and the commissaris had
his finger on the bell.

"Yes?" Mrs. Grijpstra's tousled head shouted from a
window on the second floor.

"Is your husband in, madam?"

"Oh, it's you, sir. He'll be right down."

The commissaris coughed. He could hear the woman's voice inside the house and Grijpstra's heavy foot-
steps on the narrow wooden staircase. The door opened.

"Morning, sir," Grijpstra said. "Excuse my wife, sir.
She is getting too fat to move around much and she
won't answer the door anymore. Just sits near the window and shouts a lot. Right opposite the TV, but there
won't be any TV till this afternoon."

"Never mind," the commissaris said.

"We are going to see this Bezuur fellow first, aren't
we, sir? Does he know we are coming?"

They were in the car now and Grijpstra greeted the
sleepy-eyed constable at the wheel. The constable wasn't
in uniform but sported a dark blue blazer with the
emblem of the Amsterdam Municipal Police Sports
Club embroidered on the left top pocket.

"Yes. I phoned and he will see us right now. Then
we can have lunch somewhere and see if we can raise
the two ladies on the phone. I would like to see them
later today if possible."

"Good," Grijpstra said and accepted a cigar.

"You don't mind working on a Sunday, do you,
Grijpstra?"

"No, sir. Not at all, sir."

"Shouldn't you be taking the little ones out?"

"I took the brats to the zoo only last week, sir, and today they are going to play at a friend's house. And they are not so small anymore. The littlest one is six and the other one eight."

The commissaris mumbled.

"Pardon, sir?"

"Shouldn't have asked you to come," the commissaris repeated. "You are a family man and you were up half the night. Sietsema could have come just as well, I don't think he is working on anything now anyway."

"No, sir. But Sietsema isn't on this case, sir. I am."

The commissaris smiled. "How is your oldest son, by the way? He must be eighteen, right?"

"Right sir, but there's nothing right about the boy."

"Doing badly with his studies?"

"Dropped out altogether and now he wants to leave the house. The army doesn't want him and he'll never find a job, not even if he wanted to, which he doesn't. When he leaves the house he'll be applying for national assistance, he says. I never know where he is these days. Rushing about on that little motorbike, I imagine, and smoking hash with his friends. He's sniffing too, caught him the other day. Cocaine powder."

"That's expensive," the commissaris said.

"Very."

"Any idea where he gets the money?"

"Not from me, sir."

"So?"

"I've been with the police a long time, sir."

"Dealing?"

"Everything, I think," Grijpstra said and pretended to be watching the traffic. "Dealing, motorbike stealing, straight-out burglarizing and a bit of prostitution. He doesn't like girls so he'll never be a pimp, but that's the only bad thing he'll never be."

"Prostitution?" the commissaris asked.

"He goes to the wrong pubs, the sort of places where they pick up the shopkeeper from the provinces and get him to take them to a motel."

"That's bad," the commissaris said. "Anything we can do to stop him?"

"No, sir. I am not going to hunt my own son but one of our colleagues will stumble into him and then it'll be reform school and he'll come back worse. I have written him off. So have the social workers. The boy isn't even interested in watching TV or football."

"Neither is Sergeant de Gier," the commissaris said brightly, "so there's still hope."

"De Gier has a cat to care for, and he reads. He has things to do. Flowerpots on the balcony and flute-playing and judo at least one evening a week and visiting museums on Sundays. And when a woman is after him he gives in. Sometimes anyway."

"Yes," the commissaris cackled. "He's giving in right now."

Grijpstra thought.

"Esther Rogge? Nellie didn't want him."

"Esther Rogge."

"He'll never learn," Grijpstra said gruffly. "Bloody fool he is. The woman is involved in the case."

"She's a lovely woman," the commissaris said. "A refined woman even. She'll do him good."

"You don't mind then, sir?" Grijpstra sounded relieved.

"I want to find the killer," the commissaris said, "and quickly, before he swings his ball at somebody else. The man can't be altogether sane, and he is certainly inventive. We still haven't worked out what weapon he used."

Grijpstra sighed and leaned a little further into the soft upholstery of the car. "It may be a simple case after all, sir. The man was a hawker, a street seller. They usually make a lot more money than the taxman should know about and they hide the difference in tins under the bed, or in a secret place behind the paneling, or under the floor somewhere. One of my informers told me that over a hundred thousand guilders were stolen from an old mate of his, a man selling cheese in the street. The cheese-man never reported the theft because he wasn't supposed to have that much money. If the taxman had heard about it he would have stung the poor fellow for at least half of it, so the poor sucker kept quiet and cried alone. But Abe Rogge may have wanted to defend his cache and he got killed."

"By a spiked ball swung at his face?"

"Yes," Grijpstra said, "why not? Maybe the killer is a man who is clever with his hands. A carpenter, a plumber. Maybe he made his own weapon, invented it."

"But he never took Abe's wallet," the commissaris said. "There was a lot of money in the wallet. If he came for money he wouldn't have left a few thousand right in his victim's pocket. He only had to reach for it. An inventive man, you said. Louis Zilver is inventive. Remember that figure he was trying to create out of beads and wire?"

"He threw it into a dustbin," Grijpstra said, "made a mess of it. But the idea was inventive, true."

Grijpstra looked out of the window of the car. They were in the southern part of Amsterdam now, and gigantic stone-and-steel structures blocked the sky, like enormous bricks dotted with small holes.

And they are full of people, Grijpstra thought. Little people. Little innocent people, preparing their Sunday lunch, lounging about, reading the paper, playing with their kids and with their animals, making plans for the rest of the day. He looked at his watch. Or having a late breakfast. Sunday morning, best time of the week.

The car stopped at a traffic light and he found himself staring at a balcony, populated by a complete family. Father, mother, two small children. There was a dog on the balcony too. One of the children was making the dog stand up by dangling a biscuit just above its head. The toddler and the small dog made a pretty picture. The geraniums in the flower boxes attached to the balcony's railing were in full flower.

And we are chasing a killer, Grijpstra thought.

"Louis Zilver," the comissaris said, "not a very well-adjusted young man perhaps. I had him checked out last night. He has a previous conviction, for resisting

arrest when caught making a drunken racket in the
street. Happened a few years ago. He attacked the constables who tried to put him into a patrol car. The judge
was very easy on him, a fine and a lecture. What do
you think, adjutant? Do we put him on the list of
prime suspects?"

Grijpstra's thoughts were still with the family on
the balcony. The harmonious family. The happy family.
He was wondering whether he himself, Adjutant Grijpstra, flat-footed sleuth, bogey-man of the underworld,
restless wanderer of canals, alleyways, dark cul-de-sacs,
would like to be happy, like the young healthy father
enthroned on his geranium-decorated balcony on the
second floor of a huge transparent brick, facing a main
thoroughfare.

"Grijpstra?"

"Sir," Grijpstra said. "Yes, definitely. Prime suspect.
Surely. It's all there. Motive and opportunity. Maybe
he was greedy, wanted the business for himself. Or
jealous of Rogge's interminable successes. Or he might
have wanted Esther and Abe wouldn't let him. Or he
was trying to get at Esther through Abe. But I don't
know."

"No?" the commissaris asked.

"No, sir. He's a bungler, that's what he is."

"A bungler?" the commissaris asked. "Why? His room
seemed well-organized, didn't it? Bookkeeping all neatly
stacked on a shelf. The bed was made, the floor was
clean. I am sure Esther didn't look after the room
for him; he must have done it himself. And his clothes
were washed; he even had a crease in his trousers."

"Because of Abe," Grijpstra said. "Abe pulled him
together. Before he started hanging on to Rogge he was
nothing. Dropout from university, sleeping late, drinking, fooling around with beads. He functioned because
Abe made him function. I am sure he can do nothing
on his own."

"Can't make a weapon that shoots a spiked ball, you
mean."

"Yes sir."

"Yes, yes, yes," the commissaris said.

"I think the killer may be some connection at the street market, sir, and it seems to me you are thinking the same way, or you wouldn't be pushing de Gier and Cardozo into their masquerade tomorrow. They are going to be hawkers, didn't you say so?"

"Yes," the commissaris said, and smiled.

"This is the address, sir," the constable at the wheel said.

Grijpstra hissed admiringly as he looked at the bungalow spread on a low artificial hill, sitting in the middle of at least an acre of freshly mown grass, decorated with bushes and evergreens. The gate was open and the Citroën eased itself into the driveway.

The front door of the bungalow opened as they got out of the car.

"Bezuur," the man said as he pumped the commissaris' hand. "I was waiting for you. Please come in."

8

A PUDDING for a face, Grijpstra thought, turning his head to watch Klaas Bezuur. Nobody had said anything for at least a minute. The commissaris, at the far end of the vast room, which covered almost three quarters of the modern bungalow, had made Grijpstra think of his youngest son's rag doll, a small lost object thrown into a large chair. The commissaris was in pain. Self-propelled white-hot needles were drilling into the bones of his legs. He was breathing deeply and had half-closed his eyes, fighting the temptation to close them completely. He felt very tired, he badly wanted to go to sleep. But he had to keep his mind on the case. Klaas Bezuur, the dead man's friend, was facing him.

A pudding, Grijpstra thought again. They have dropped a pudding on a human skull, a pudding of blubbery fat. The fat has oozed down, from the cranium downward. It covered the cheek-bones and then it slowly dripped down to the jaws and clung to the chin.

Bezuur was sitting on the edge of his chair, straight up. His round belly hung over his belt and Grijpstra could see folds of flesh, hairy flesh, embedding the navel. The man was sweating. The sweat from his armpits was staining his striped tailor-made silk shirt. Bezuur's face gleamed and drops were forming on the low forehead, joining each other in miniature streams, gliding down, hesitating near the small pudgy nose. It was very hot, of course. Grijpstra was sweating too.

A big man, Grijpstra thought. Over six feet, he must weigh a ton. He'll eat a hundred guilders a day, easily. Bowlsful of cashew nuts proboably, and shrimps, and a bucket or two of potatoes, or spaghetti, and a loaf of bread thrown in, bread covered with fried mushrooms and smoked eel and thick slices of ham.

Bezuur reached out and grabbed a bottle of beer out of a carton placed near his chair. He broke off the cap and filled his glass. The thick foam rose quickly and flowed down the sides of the glass, spilling onto the thick rug.

"More beer, gentlemen?"

The commissaris shook his head. Grijpstra nodded. Bezuur tore the cap off another bottle. More foam was sucked into the rug. "Here you are, adjutant."

They looked each other in the eye and raised their glasses, grunting simultaneously. Bezuur drained his glass. Grijpstra took a carefully measured sip; it was his third glass. Bezuur had had six since they came into the room. Grijpstra put the glass down gingerly.

"He is dead, the bastard," Bezuur said, and viciously replaced the glass on a marble-topped side table. It cracked and he looked at it dolefully. "The silly stupid bastard. Or perhaps he was clever. He always said that death is a trip and he liked traveling. He used to talk a lot about death, even when he was a boy. He talked a lot and he read a lot. Later he drank a lot too. He was an alcoholic when he was seventeen years old. Did anybody tell you?"

"No," Grijpstra said. "You tell us."

"An alcoholic," Bezuur said again. "Became one when we entered the university. We were always together, at school and at the university. We passed our high school examinations when we were sixteen. Wonderkids we were. We never worked but we always passed. I was good at mathematics and he was good at languages. When we did work we worked together. A deadly team we were; nobody and nothing could tear us apart. We only worked when we came to an examination and then we would only put in the bare minimum. It was pride, I think. Showing off. We would pretend we weren't listening at classes but we soaked it all up, and we remembered the stuff too. And we made secret notes, on scraps of paper; we didn't have notebooks like the other kids. And no homework, homework was for the birds. We read. But he read more than I did and at the university he began to drink."

"He did?" Grijpstra asked.

"Yes."

Bezuur's hand shot out and another bottle lost its cap. He looked at the cracked glass, and turned around to look at the kitchen door. He must have had more glasses in the kitchen but it was too far, and he drank from the bottle, tossing the cap on the floor. He looked at Grijpstra's glass but it was still half full.

"I think he was drinking a bottle a day. Jenever. He would drink any brand as long as it was cold. One day he couldn't get his pants on in the morning, his hands trembled too much. He thought it was funny but I worried and made him see a doctor who told him to lay off. He did too."

"Really?" Grijpstra asked. "He stopped drinking straight off? Just like that?"

"Yes. He was clever. He didn't want to be a drunk; it would complicate his routine."

"Stopped drinking straight off, hey," Grijpstra said, shaking his head.

"I told you he was clever," Bezuur said. "He knew it would be difficult to break the habit so he did something drastic. He disappeared for a while, three months I think it was. Went to work on a farm. When he came back he was off it. Later he began drinking again but then he knew when to stop. He would cut out at the third or fourth glass and drink soft stuff."

"Beer?"

"Beer is not so soft. No, lemonades, homemade. He would fuss about, squeezing the fruit, adding sugar. With Abe everything had to be dead right."

Bezuur tipped the bottle again but it was empty and he slammed it on the table. The bottle cracked. He glared at it.

"You seem a little upset," Grijpstra said.

Bezuur was staring at the wall behind Grijpstra's chair. "Yes," he said, "I am upset. So the bastard died. How the hell did he manage that? I spoke to Zilver on the phone. He reckons they threw a ball at him, a metal ball, but nobody can find it. Is that right?"

He was still staring at the wall behind Grijpstra's chair and Grijpstra turned around. There was a painting on the wall, a portrait of a lady. The lady was wearing a long skirt of some velvety material, a hat with a veil, an elaborate necklace, and nothing else. She had very full breasts with the nipples turned upward. The face was quiet, a delicate face with dreaming eyes and lips which opened in the beginning of a smile.

"Beautiful," Grijpstra said.

"My wife."

Grijpstra looked around the room.

Bezuur laughed, the laugh sounded bubbly and gushy, as if a pipe had suddenly burst and water was flowing down the wall.

"My ex-wife, I should say, perhaps, but the divorce isn't through yet. She left me some months ago now and her lawyers are squeezing me and my lawyers are having a lovely time, writing lots of little notes at a guilder a word."

"Any children?"

"One, but not mine. The fruit of a previous relationship. Some fruit, a little overripe apple, and stupid too—but what do I care, she went too."

"So you are alone."

Bezuur laughed again and the commissaris looked up.

He wished the man wouldn't laugh. He had found a
way of putting up with the pain in his legs but Bezuur's
merriment shook his concentration and the pain attacked again.

"No," Bezuur said, and stretched his right arm. The
arm swept in a half circle.

"Girlfriends," Grijpstra said, and nodded.

"Yes. Girls. I used to go to them but now they come
here. It's easier. I am getting too heavy to run about."

He looked at the floor, stamping his foot on the sodden rug. "Bah. Beer. Something to do for the cleaning
boys. You can't get charwomen anymore you know, not
even if you pay them in gold bars. Some cleaning
platoon comes here on weekdays, old men in white uniforms. They have a truck and the biggest vacuum cleaner
you ever saw. Whip through the whole place in an hour.
But the girls come on Fridays or Saturdays and they
leave a mess and I sit in it. Bah."

His arm made a sweeping movement again and
Grijpstra followed the movement. He counted five
empty champagne bottles. Someone had forgotten her
lipstick on the couch. There was a stain on the white
wall, just below the painting of Bezuur's wife.

"Turtle soup," Bezuur said. "Silly bitch lost her bal-
ance and the soup hit the wall. Good thing it missed
the painting."

"Who did the painting?"

"You like it?"

"Yes," Grijpstra said. "Yes. I think it is very well
done. Like that picture of the two men in a small boat
I saw on Abe Rogge's wall."

Bezuur looked at the carton next to his chair, took
out a bottle but put it back again.

"Two men in a boat? You saw that painting too, eh?
Same artist. Old friends of ours, a Russian Jew born in
Mexico, used to go boating with us and he came to the
house. Interesting fellow, but he wandered off again. I
think he is in Israel now."

"Who were the two men in the boat?"

"Abe and me," Bezuur said heavily. "Abe and me

Two friends. The Mexican fellow said that we belonged together, he saw it that night. We were on the big lake, the boat was anchored and we had taken the dinghy into the harbor. We came back late that night. The sea was fluorescent and the Mexican was wandering about on deck. He left the next day, he should have stayed a few more days, but he was so inspired by what he saw that night that he had to get back to his studio to paint it. Abe bought the painting and I commissioned this one later. That Mexican was very expensive, even if you were his friend, but he was pretty good."

"Friends," the commissaris said. "Close friends. You were close friends with Abe, weren't you, Mr. Bezuur?"

"Was," Bezuur said, and there was the same blubbery note in his voice again, but now he seemed close to tears. "The bastard is dead."

"You were close friends right up to yesterday?"

"No," Bezuur said. "Lost touch. Went his way, I went my way. I have a big business now and no time to play about on the street market, but I enjoyed it while it lasted."

"When did you each go your own way?"

"Wasshit matter?" Bezuur said, and that was all they could get out of him for a while. He was crying now, and had opened another bottle, slopping half of it on the floor. The fit took a few minutes.

"Shorry," Bezuur said.

"That's all right," the commissaris said, and rubbed his legs. "We understand. And I am sorry we are bothering you."

"What did Mr. Rogge and yourself study at the university?" Grijpstra asked. Bezuur looked up, there seemed to be some strength in him again and he was no longer slurring his words.

"French. We studied French."

"But you weren't so good at languages. Didn't you say so before?" the commissaris asked.

"Not too bad either," Bezuur said. "Good enough. French is a logical language, very exact. Maybe I would have preferred science but it would have meant breaking from Abe, I wasn't ready for that then."

"Did you study hard?"

"Same way we got through high school, in my case anyway. Abe was more enthusiastic. He read everything he could find at the university library, starting at the top shelf on the left and finishing on the bottom shelf on the right. If the books didn't interest him he would flip the pages, reading a little here and there but often he would read the whole book. I just read what he selected for me, books he talked about."

"And what else did you two do?"

Bezuur was staring at the portrait and the commissaris had to ask again.

"What else? Oh, we ran about. And I had a big boat in those days; we'd go sailing on the lakes. And we traveled. Abe had a little truck and we went to France and North Africa and once I talked my father into buying us tickets on an old tramp which went to Haiti in the Caribbean. The language is French over there and I said we needed the experience for our study."

"Your father paid for Abe's ticket as well? Didn't Abe have any money himself?"

"He had some. German love-money. The Germans paid up after the war, you know, and they had killed both his parents. He got quite a bit; so did Esther. Abe knew how to handle money. He was doing a little business on the side. He was buying and selling antique weapons in those days."

"Weapons?" the commissaris asked. "He didn't happen to have a good-day, did he?"

"No," Bezuur said, when the question had got through to him. "No, no, cavalry sabers and bayonets, that sort of stuff. You think he was killed with a good-day?"

"Never mind," the commissaris said. "Did he ever live out of your pocket?"

Bezuur shook his head. "No, not really. He accepted that ticket to Haiti but he made up for it in other ways. He only relied on himself. He would borrow money sometimes but he always paid up on time and later,

when I was lending him big money, he paid full bank
interest. The interest was his idea, I never asked for it
but he said I had a right to it."

"Why didn't he borrow from the bank?"

"He didn't want his transactions on record. He borrowed cash and he paid cash. He was pretending to be
a small hawker, a fellow who lived off his stall."

The commissaris looked at Grijpstra and Grijpstra
asked the next question.

"Why did you both drop out of the university?"

Bezuur looked at his beer bottle and shook it. "Yes,
we dropped out, right at the end. Abe's idea, that was.
He said the degree would be pure silliness, it would
qualify us to become schoolteachers. We had learned
all we wanted to learn anyway. We went into business
instead."

"The street market?"

"Yes. I started importing from the communist countries. In Rumania a lot of people speak French and we
went there to see what we could find. The East Bloc
started exporting cheaply in those days, to get hard cur-
rency. You could pick up all sorts of bargains. They
offered wool and buttons and zippers, so we found ourselves in the street market. The big stores wouldn't
buy at first and we had to unload the goods. We made
good money, but then my dad died and left the road-
working machinery business so I had to switch."

"Were you sorry?"

"Yes," Bezuur said and drained the bottle. "I am still
sorry. Wrong choice, but there was nothing else to do.
There's more money in bulldozers than in colored
string."

"You cared about money?"

Bezuur nodded gravely. "I did."

"You still do?"

Bezuur didn't appear to hear.

"One last question." Grijpstra said brightly. "About
this party last night. When did it begin and when did it
end?"

Bezuur scratched the stubbles on his bloated cheeks.

The small eyes looked sly in their greasy sockets. "Alibi, hey? And I don't even know when Abe was killed. Zilver didn't tell me. Party started at about nine in the evening. I can get the girls to testify if you like. I should have their names and phone numbers somewhere."

"Callgirls?"

"Yes. Sure. Whores."

He was looking through the pockets of a jacket which he had taken from the couch. "Here you are, telephone numbers, you can copy them. The names are fancy, of course. Minette and Alice, they call themselves, but they answer their phones if you need them. Better try tomorrow, they'll be asleep now. I had them driven home in a taxi at five o'clock this morning. They had a gallon of champagne each, and another gallon of food."

Grijpstra jotted down the numbers. "Thank you."

"Excuse me, sir," the constable said. He had been standing in the open door for some time.

"Yes, constable?"

"You are wanted on the radio sir."

"Well, we have finished here, I think," the commissaris said. "Thank you for your hospitality, Mr. Bezuur. Contact me if you think I should know something which you haven't mentioned now. Here is my card. We would like to solve the case."

"I'll let you know," Bezuur said and got up. "God knows I'll be thinking about it all the time. I have done nothing else since Zilver phoned."

"I thought you were having a little party here, sir," Grijpstra said, keeping his voice flat.

"I can think while I have a party," Bezuur said, taking the commissaris' card.

"Another dead body in the Straight Tree Ditch, sir," the female constable from the radio room said. "Water Police found it. It was dangling from a rope tied to a tree, half in the water and partly hidden by a moored boat. The Water Police suggested we should contact you. They had seen the telegrams* reporting the other murder last night. Same area, sir. Sergeant de Gier is there now. He's got Detective-Constable Cardozo with him. They are in their car waiting for instructions. Would you like to speak to them, sir?"

"Put them on," the commissaris said, gloomily looking at the microphone which Grijpstra was holding for him.

"Cardozo here, sir."

"We are on our way to you now," the commissaris said, nodding to the constable at the wheel who started the car. The constable pointed at the roof and raised his eyebrows. "Yes," the commissaris mouthed silently. The siren began to howl and the blue light flashed as the car shot away. "Anything you can tell us at this stage, Cardozo?"

"Sergeant de Gier knows the dead person, sir. An old man dressed up as a lady. Used to be on the force, sir." Cardozo's voice had gone up, as if he was framing a question.

"Yes, I know her, Cardozo. How did she die?"

"Knife in his back sir. He must have been killed in a public telephone booth here; we found a track. He was dragged across the street and dumped into the canal. The killer used a short rope, strung under the corpse's armpits and attached to an old elm tree. The rope didn't kill him. The knife did."

"Do you have the knife?"

"No, sir. But the doctor said it was a knife wound. Penetrated the heart from the back. A long knife."

"When did she die?"

"Early this morning, sir, the doctor thinks."

"We'll be there soon."

"The Water Police want to have the corpse, sir. Can they take it? It's quiet now but the riots may start any minute again and we are blocking the street with our cars."

"Yes," the commissaris said tiredly, looking at a city bus which was trying to get out of the Citroën's way. The constable at the wheel was attempting to pass the bus and several cars were coming from the opposite direction. The siren was screaming ominously directly above them. The commissaris put a restraining hand on the constable's shoulder and the car slowed down obediently.

"They can have the body, Cardozo. Over and out."

Grijpstra was watching the oncoming traffic too and sighed happily when the Citroën nosed back behind the bus. "Bloody fool," he said to the constable. "What are you trying to do, be a hero?"

The constable didn't hear him. The bus pulled to the side of the road, having finally found a spot free of cyclists, and the Citroën jumped off again, careening wildly.

"Oh, shit," Grijpstra said softly.

"Quite," the commissaris said.

"Pardon, sir?"

"That wasn't very clever of me," the commissaris said, "asking that poor old lady to be on the force again. I might as well have shot her on the spot."

9

"You'll have to get out of here, sir," de Gier said. He had gotten into the car as Grijpstra got out. "The riots will be starting all over today. I don't know what's gotten into these people but they are thronging about again and warming each other up. The riot police will be out any minute now."

The commissaris was leaning back into his seat.

"Are you all right, sir?"

"No," the commissaris said softly, so that de Gier had to bend over to hear him. "It's this pain. It's been with me all day and it isn't getting any better. Riots, you say. The riot police will only make it worse. We don't want a show of force, sergeant."

"No, sir. But what else can we do? They'll be throwing bricks and there are some bulldozers in the New-market Square, and cranes and machines. They can destroy a fortune's worth in a few minutes."

"Yes," the commissaris said softly.

A platoon of riot police came tramping past. The commissaris shuddered.

"There they are," de Gier said.

"I hate that sound, tramping boots. We heard it during the war. All the time. A stupid sound. We ought to
be more intelligent now."

"Yes, sir," de Gier said. He was watching the commissaris' gray tired face. A spasm moved both cheeks
and the commissaris' yellowish teeth were bared for a
moment in a grin of agony. "You'd better take him
home, constable," de Gier said to the driver. The constable nodded.

"In a minute," the commissaris said. "Tell me what
happened, sergeant. Is the corpse still here? Did you
manage to organize yourself for tomorrow's market-
ing?"

"We'll take care of that later today sir. I was at home
when the Water Police telephoned. I came straight out.
Cardozo happened to phone as I was leaving, so he
came out as well. I have had the corpse moved to the
mortuary. There may be street fighting here soon and
I didn't want them to trample all over it. Cardozo said
that it would be O.K. with you. He spoke to you on the
radio."

"Yes, yes. Did you find out anything? And have you
taken Miss Rogge home?"

"Esther Rogge should be home by now, sir, she
caught a bus."

"She stayed at your apartment all night, de Gier?"

"Yes, sir."

"I see. And the corpse, did you get any clues?"

"Just what Cardozo must have told you, sir. A knife
killed him. I think he was trying to contact you by telephone, in the booth over there. It must have been early
this morning, around four o'clock, the doctor said.
Maybe he saw the killer walking about in the street
here. Perhaps he thought he was safe, dressed up like an
old lady, and all. He got into the telephone booth and
got a knife in his back."

"Yes," the commissaris said. "She was trying to telephone me but she didn't get through. Poor Elizabeth.
She must have been dialing my number as the killer

knifed her. Elizabeth was a 'she,' de Gier, you shouldn't refer to her as a 'he.' She was a nice old lady, and courageous too. I should never have asked her to help us. She should have been in bed last night, with Tabby warming her old feet."

"She wasn't," de Gier said. "She was right here, watching the killer return to the scene of the crime. And I should have been here too. And Grijpstra. She was dragged from that booth to the water; we found blood traces on the cobblestones. The killer had all the time in the world. He didn't just dump the body. If he did it would have floated and somebody would have found it almost immediately. He tied it up with a bit of string. It's amazing the Water Police found it so quickly. It was well hidden between the quay and that houseboat over there."

"So you didn't notice anything special, did you? Apart from the blood traces?"

"Yes, sir. The knots in the string. They were professional knots, made by a sailor or an experienced fisherman. Which reminds me, sir . . ."

"Yes?"

"I think I know a little more about the spiked rubber ball which killed Abe Rogge."

"Tell me."

"I saw some kids playing with a ball attached to an elastic string once, sir. The string was held by a weight placed on the street. I think the ball which killed Rogge was attached to a string too. The killer pulled it back afterward, which explains why we didn't find it. And I think the killer wasn't in the street; he was on the roof of the old houseboat moored opposite Rogges' house. Perhaps he had hidden himself behind the chimney. You can see it over there, sir." De Gier pointed to the other side of the Straight Tree Ditch.

"Yes," the commissaris said. "So the riot police in the street didn't see him maybe. That's what you mean, don't you? But there were riot police patrolling this side of the canal too. Shouldn't they have seen him?"

"He must have been quick, sir. Hid himself in the

houseboat, sneaked through one of its windows at the
right moment, threw the ball, pulled it back, sneaked
back into the boat's window and disappeared later when
the constables were at the other end of the street. They
would have let him through easily enough. He probably looked like an ordinary citizen and they wouldn't
have thought that he was a rioter. I think they took him
for someone who lived in the street and who had come
out to do a little shopping or go somewhere."

"The killer could have been a woman," the commissaris said. "Abe Rogge had a lot of girlfriends. A
jealous woman or a humiliated woman. I am supposed
to see two of them today. You gave me the names and
addresses, remember? I am sure they are both young
and strong and capable of throwing balls."

De Gier shook his head.

"You don't think the killer might have been a woman, sergeant?"

"Could be, sir, why not? But I can't understand the
deadly aim of the ball. Even from the roof of that
houseboat there's quite a distance to cover and the ball
hit Rogge smack in the face. Now if the ball had been
shot . . . I think we are dealing with a hellish machine,
sir."

The commissaris grimaced.

"Well, it could be, couldn't it, sir?"

The commissaris nodded.

"But a machine which throws or shoots a ball makes
a sound. Or would it have used a spring perhaps? A
crossbow maybe? But then there is still some sort of
twang. A loud sound, I would say. The patrolling constables should have heard it."

"A person on the roof of a houseboat handling some
strange noisy device while riot police are close . . ." The
commissaris' voice sounded doubtful.

"Perhaps not," de Gier agreed.

"But I agree with your thought of the ball being connected to string, elastic or otherwise," the commissaris
said. "Very clever to think of that, sergeant. You
started off right, all you have to do now is continue

your line of reasoning. I'll help. And so should Grijpstra and Cardozo. It's probably quite simple. Everything is simple once you understand it." He grimaced again.

"Something funny sir?"

The commissaris groaned and rubbed his thighs. "Yes. I was thinking of something which happened the other day. My wife bought a newfangled type of folding chair and brought it home. She had forgotten how it worked and I fussed with it for a while but it only squeezed my hand. Then the neighbor's daughter came in. She is retarded but her lack of brain didn't stop her from having a go at the damned chair and she had it standing up in no time at all. I asked her to show me how she had done it but she didn't know. Evidently she could only solve a problem very quickly, without thinking about it."

"You think this killing device is like your folding chair, sir?"

"Perhaps," the commissaris said. "Maybe we should just concentrate on the problem and the solution will pop up. Thinking might take too long. We haven't got much time."

"Yes," de Gier said. "You are looking ill, sir, shouldn't you go home?"

"I'll go home now. I want you to check out two women sometime this afternoon or tonight. Grijpstra has their names and telephone numbers. They are call-girls and they were with Klaas Bezuur from about nine o'clock last night till about five o'clock this morning. Grijpstra!"

Grijpstra came ambling up.

"Sir?"

"I am going home for a while, I don't feel so well. Telephone the two ladies we are supposed to see today; set up appointments for late this afternoon or this evening. Once you have set up the appointments you can contact my driver and he'll pick you up and then you can come and fetch me. It would be best if one of the girls is available before dinner and the other after dinner. That way you and I can eat together sometime. I want to make up for calling you out today."

Grijpstra brought out his notebook and wrote down the names and addresses of the two girls.

"Yes, sir. They used to be Mr. Rogge's girlfriends, right, sir?"

"Right."

"Constable," the commissaris shouted.

"Sir."

"Home," the commissaris whispered. It was all he could say. He was almost fainting with pain.

Grijpstra found de Gier contemplating a tree trunk. The lithe body of the sergeant swayed slightly as he stood, hands folded on his back, staring moodily at the elm's green bark.

Cardozo was watching the sergeant too. "Don't disturb him," Cardozo said, holding Grijpstra back. "He is busy. He is swaying. Look."

"So he is," the adjutant said.

"He isn't Jewish, is he?" Cardozo asked.

"Not that I know of," Grijpstra said. "Although, yes, I think he told me once that he has a Jewish grandmother."

"You see," Cardozo said. "He is Jewish. If his grandmother was Jewish his mother was too and that makes him a Jew. It goes via the female line, very wisely. Nobody ever knows who his father was but you can be sure about your mother. And Jews sway, they always sway. When they have a problem, that is, or when they are concentrating on something. They do it during prayer. Back and forth, back and forth. The Spanish Inquisition used to catch us because we swayed. We couldn't help ourselves. And they'd burn us. A strange habit, isn't it?"

"No," Grijpstra said. "The sergeant is an ordinary man, like me. He is swaying because he feels like swaying. Not because he has Jewish blood. Maybe he hasn't got any, maybe somebody else told me he had a Jewish grandmother."

"Holland had only one philosopher," Cardozo said, speaking very slowly, articulating every syllable. "Spinoza. He was a Jew, and he didn't even write in Dutch, he wrote in Latin."

"Why didn't he write in Dutch?"

"He couldn't do it. Have you ever tried to express subtle thoughts in Dutch?"

"I never have subtle thoughts," Grijpstra said, "but it's about time we had some."

"Yes," de Gier said and stopped swaying. "You'd better do something for a change, Cardozo, instead of proving the superiority of your race. The commissaris wants you to help me. Listen."

He explained his theory about the weapon.

"A ball and an elastic thread," Cardozo said. "Yes."

"So how did it manage to hit Rogge square in the face, from that distance?"

Cardozo folded his hands on his back, closed his eyes and began to sway. After a while he opened his eyes again.

"I'll tell you, sergeant, when I know. It'll come to me. But not when you rush me."

"Bah," de Gier said. He remembered how he had helped the Water Police constables to haul the old lady's soggy corpse from the canal. He also remembered the expression on the corpse's face. She had been killed while she was trying to pass on some information. The face had looked eager, and also rather sweet. She had been about to speak to the commissaris, her old and close friend. She had looked coy. Coy and eager.

Grijpstra's hand was on the sergeant's shoulder.

"Let's go," Grijpstra said. "You and I have things to do. You have to check out two whores and I have to telephone some nice ladies. But we have a little time. Stop looking at that tree, it has nothing to say to you. Fancy tying a corpse to a tree and then throwing it into the water. I am going to have a drink, care to join me?"

"Can I come too?" Cardozo asked.

"No. You are too young. We are going to visit a friend of mine and you won't be able to work once you have seen her. You need your strength for tomorrow. Aren't you two going to be street sellers tomorrow?"

"Then de Gier can't go either," Cardozo said. "He'll also be a street seller."

"You're right," Grijpstra said. "I'll go alone."

"Nellie?" de Gier asked.

"Yes." Grijpstra was grinning. "I'll go and see her by myself. She'll change my mood. Some day this is. Another corpse. Two corpses too many. Amsterdam is a quiet city. Holland has the lowest crime rate in the world. You went to that lecture too, didn't you? That slob should be with us now. Silly bald-headed dwarf. I can't stand criminologists. Statistics, that's all they know. When that kid got raped and slaughtered last year he said that the percentage of children killed by rapists is so low that it is almost negligible. You remember what that boy looked like when he was found?"

"According to statistics we'll have another five corpses this year," Cardozo said. "There's nothing we can do about it. They'll happen."

"The hell with you both," Grijpstra said and stamped off.

De Gier ran after him.

"Hey," Cardozo shouted.

"He's not going to drink by himself," de Gier shouted back. "Come and pick me up tomorrow at eight-thirty, and make sure that van is in order and that you have the merchandise."

"Yes, sergeant," Cardozo said loudly. "I hope you choke on your drink," he added softly.

10

"HELLO," de Gier said.

"Hello-oh," a sugary voice answered.

"Minette?"

"Yes, darling."

"I am not your darling," de Gier said and frowned at Nellie, who was watching him from the other end of the small bar. Nellie was smiling delightedly and Grijpstra was grinning. Grijpstra had taken off his coat and tie and was sitting in a corner of the room, near a window which he had opened and which showed a view of a small courtyard where a row of sparrows were lolling about on a wall, their tiny beaks open and their wings half-spread. Grijpstra was puffing and wiping his face with a large dirty white handkerchief. He looked happy, in spite of the heat. He had set up the two appointments with Rogge's girlfriends and would be off in a little while to fetch the commissaris, and meanwhile he had nothing to do but watch de Gier.

"I am not your darling," de Gier was saying. "I am Detective-Sergeant de Gier, Amsterdam Municipal

Police, and I am coming out to see you to ask you a few questions. Nothing serious, strictly routine."

"Police?" the sugary voice asked. "They are darlings too. I have a nice client who is a police officer. Maybe you are like him. When are you coming to see me, darling? Right now?"

"Right now," de Gier said and made a face at the telephone, "and I want to see your friend Alice too. Would you ask her to come over to your place? I have her telephone number here and the first three numbers are the same as yours. She must live close to you."

"But surely," Minette said. "She lives in the same building, two floors up. I'll ask her to come and we'll do a double number for you."

"No," de Gier said, "don't put yourself out, dear. I just want some simple answers to some simple questions. I'll be there in fifteen minutes. Put some clothes on."

Grijpstra chuckled and de Gier made a gesture to shut him up.

"What sort of clothes, darling? I have a nice uniform with shiny buttons and leather boots, and a little whip. Or would you prefer me to dress up in lace? Or my black evening dress perhaps? It has a beautiful zipper and it comes off if you . . ."

"NO," de Gier almost shouted. "What's the address?"

"Alkemalaan Five-O-Three, darling, don't shout at me." The voice was still dripping with sweetness.

"I'll be there," de Gier said.

"An idiot," Minette said to herself, as she daintily replaced the dark red plastic telephone on her bedside table, "and rude too. Now what does *he* want? He wouldn't be hunting whores, would he? That other policeman also said he wanted to ask questions, but he came for the usual thing and stayed the night. They are all idiots."

"Afternoon," de Gier said. "I am Sergeant de Gier. I phoned about a quarter of an hour ago. Are you Minette?"

"No, honey," the small girl said. "I am Alice, Minette is waiting for you inside. Come in, dear."

She put a hand on his arm and tugged gently. "My," she sighed, "aren't you handsome!"

"Yes," de Gier said. "I am a beautiful man." He looked into the smiling eyes and noted they were green. Cat's eyes. The face was triangular, like a praying mantis'. He had been looking at a color photograph of a praying mantis in a book he had found in the Public Library. The insect had looked weirdly attractive, the materialization of a subconscious fear with a lovely face but with long arms and claws. A predatory insect, the caption had said. An entity to be careful with.

The girl turned and he followed her into the small hall. A little girl, she wouldn't be much more than five feet high, but well shaped and well dressed in short velvet pants and a loose flowing blouse. Her bare feet were tiny. An imp, a prancing imp. He guessed her to be in her late twenties but the smooth face hadn't shown signs of wear and tear. Maybe she hadn't been in the game too long. He admired the round tight bottom and the black glossy hair, done up in a bun.

"Now *that* is Minette," Alice said, turning around and stepping back, so that he would enter the room ahead of her. "Here's your sergeant, Minette."

"Woo," Minette said. "Isn't he lovely?"

De Gier felt relieved. Minette was nothing special. A plump girl, rather wide in the hips and with a painted doll's face. Minette sat on a low settee, dressed in a wrap which slipped a little; one breast was visible. De Gier shuddered imperceptibly. The breast looked like the gelatin puddings his mother used to serve on birthdays. They came on a white plate, dripping with a thick cream sauce.

"Take your coat off, sergeant," Minette said in the same voice she had used on the telephone. "You were so abrupt when you rang up. Relax, that's what this place is for. Have a drink, come and sit next to me. What would you like? Get him a beer, Alice. We have some really cold beer in the fridge."

"No," de Gier said. "No drink. I am working. Thanks."

"Have a cigar," Minette said. "Do we still have those long thick cigars, Alice? They were in a big box, with an Indian on the lid, remember?"

Alice brought the box, opened it, put it on a low table next to the corner chair, which de Gier had chosen judging it to be the safest place in the room, and sat down on the carpet, within touching distance of his leg.

"You will have a cigar, won't you, sergeant?"

"Yes," de Gier said. "Please."

The small white hand touched the box, slid over it and picked out a cigar. She caressed it, looking at him languidly, and then rapidly peeled off its plastic skin and licked its end, darting the tip of her tongue in and out. Her small regular teeth showed when she saw that he was watching her. Her long eyelashes came down slowly and then, smiling wickedly, she stuck the cigar into her mouth, turned it around and bit off its end.

"Here you are, sergeant." She lit a match.

"Yes," de Gier said, "thanks. You two girls were with a Mr. Bezuur last night we were told."

"It's hot in here," Alice said. "The air conditioner is on the blink. They keep on fiddling with it but it never works when you want it to. You should get a new one, Minette. Do you mind if I take off my blouse, sergeant?"

She took it off before he could say anything. She wore nothing underneath. The breasts were pretty, very small and firm. She stretched and untied her hair, which flowed down her shoulders, and she adjusted the strands so that her nipples were covered. De Gier stared.

"Yes," he said. "It's rather hot in here. Outside too. Putting the windows down doesn't help much either. Now how long were you two with Mr. Bezuur, yesterday? Do you remember the exact times? When did you get to his house and when did you leave?"

"Bezuur?" Alice asked. "Who is Bezuur?"

"That's Klaas, of course," Minette said. "The fat fellow. You were all over him all night, remember?"

"Oh," Alice said. "The piggy man. *You* were all over

him, not me. I only danced about while he drank, and ate. He ate a whole ham. Bah. I am glad he wasn't pawing *me*. Why don't you get some of your clothes off, sergeant? I can sit on your lap, you'll hardly feel my weight."

"You don't need me in here," Minette said and pouted. "Do you want me to go into the other room?"

"No," de Gier said quickly, "no, no. Stay right here, and I am not taking my clothes off either. For God's sake, can't you two answer a simple question? When did you get to his house and when did you leave?"

"Now, now," Alice said, and moved closer. "Don't be uptight, sergeant. We won't make you pay, you are safe in here. Nobody will mind if you stay an hour. It isn't the right day for work, is it?"

"WHEN . . ." de Gier asked, and half-rose from his chair.

"We got there about nine last night and we left early this morning. Around five o'clock it was, I think. A taxi took us home."

"And Bezuur was with you all the time?"

"Sure."

"Weren't you asleep some of the time?"

"He was there while I slept," Minette said. "Right next to me."

"Sure?"

"Yes. He put his fat leg on me, I couldn't get it off. It stopped the circulation in my ankle and I had to massage it."

De Gier looked down. Alice had been inching herself toward him and was now rubbing herself against his leg.

"Yes," she said. "He was there. I was asleep on the couch some of the time but I saw him when I woke up. He was there just like you are here now. Sit back, sergeant, I am going to sit on your lap."

"No," de Gier said, and got up.

She followed him to the door. He was standing with his back against the wall, holding his notebook.

"I want your full name and Minette's name. I'll have to write a report."

"Is that piggy man in any sort of trouble?" Alice was standing very close again.

"Not really. We just want to know where he was last night."

She waited while he was making his notes, gave him their names and dates of birth.

"Profession?" de Gier asked.

"You know!" Alice said. "We are callgirls."

"Prostitutes," de Gier wrote down. "I've got to go now. Thanks for the information."

"Come back," Alice whispered quickly. "I live two floors up," number five-seven-four. Give me a ring first. I won't charge you."

"Sure," de Gier said and slipped through the door.

"Like hell," he said a little later, cruelly pushing the gear lever of the Volkswagen. Like bloody hell, a policeman-friend to help her out when she gets into trouble. But she made me feel randy, the little bitch. Just the sort of thing for a day like this.

He had to stop for a traffic light and gloomily watched a big Mercedes which had pulled up next to the Volkswagen. There were two middle-aged men in the back of the car, dressed in suits and ties. They were both smoking cigars. De Gier saw one of them blow out a little cloud of smoke, which disappeared immediately, sucked away by the air conditioning in the car. He looked at the soggy end of his own cigar, and tossed it out of the window, watching it spark as it hit the tarmac. The driver of the Mercedes winked at him. He had pushed his cap to the back of his head and was loosening his tie.

"Hot, eh?" he asked.

De Gier nodded.

The two men in the back of the car were laughing about something.

"Your passengers are cool enough," de Gier said.

"They are cool," the driver said, indicating the glass partitioning with his thumb. "I am not."

The light changed and the Mercedes accelerated.

"Bounders," de Gier thought. "Two bounders and one little sucker to whizz 'em around."

He was thinking about Alice again. Grijpstra had his Nellie. He forced himself to think about something else. He saw the spiked ball, trying to visualize its flight as it approached Abe Rogge's window. Someone was directing the ball, using a device. But what was it? He tried to visualize the device but it blurred as he focused.

11

THE COMMISSARIS looked at the young woman who, red-eyed, perched on a highbacked chair, was studying a stain on the wallpaper. They had dispensed with courtesies and he would have to make an opening.

"We were informed that you were friendly with Abe Rogge, miss. Perhaps you can tell us something about him. Any information will help. We know a little about the way he was, but not enough. Someone went to a lot of trouble to kill him. There usually is a strong connection between killer and victim. Perhaps you can help us to find out what bound the two together."

"Yes," the woman said, and sniffled. "I understand. Poor Abe. How did he die? I didn't know until the police phoned me this morning. I didn't dare to phone Esther. She must be very upset."

Grijpstra gave her an abridged version of what the police knew. He left out the gory details.

"Horrible," the woman said.

She calmed down after a while. Her two visitors looked harmless enough and were sipping coffee and

smoking cigars, careful to tip their ash into the saucers
of their cups. She remembered that she hadn't put an
ashtray on the table and got up to fetch one. The two
men didn't look out of place in the small modern flat
on the top floor of an apartment building. The commissaris commented on the view. He identified some
of the church towers and when he made a mistake, she
corrected him.

"Yes," she said. "I understand now. You have come
to me because I was his girlfriend, or one of his girlfriends rather. I didn't mind, not very much anyway.
Abe could be charming, he knew how to flatter me,
and perhaps I didn't want him all for myself. I am
reasonably content with my routine. Abe would have
upset it if he had moved in. It wasn't just sex either;
he often came to talk, about books or about films he
had seen and he took me out sometimes."

"What was he like?" the commissaris asked.

"Crazy."

"How do you mean, miss?" Grijpstra asked.

"Crazy," she repeated.

"In what way?" the commissaris asked. "He didn't
pull faces or jump about on all fours, did he?"

"No, no. How can I explain? He had an unusual idea
of values. Most people have set values, or no values at
all. Abe seemed to change his values all the time, but
without being weak. He thought from an angle nobody
could grasp. I didn't understand him either and I often
tried."

The commissaris had come a little forward in his
chair. "That isn't enough, miss. You have to tell us a
little more. I can't see the man; we only met him as a
corpse, you see. You knew him well . . ."

"Yes. I'll try. Well . . . he was courageous. Perhaps
that's the word. No fear, no fear of anything. When he
thought of something he did it or tried to do it and
most of the things he did seemed absolutely pointless.
They weren't getting him anywhere but he didn't mind.
Perhaps he didn't want to get anywhere. You have
heard about his business, have you?"

"Beads," the commissaris said, "and wool."

"Yes. Funny things. He could have been a big businessman, a manager of a large firm perhaps but he preferred to shout on the market, on the Albert Cuyp street market. I wouldn't believe it at first, not until I went there. A showman, hypnotizing the poor housewives, telling them they were creative, and admiring the ugly sweaters and the horrible dolls they had made out of his yarn. It was pathetic to see those inane dumpy women swarming around his stall. And he almost graduated in French. I knew him at the university; he was the best student of our year, the pride of the professors. His essays were brilliant, anything he did was original, but . . ."

"You make him sound as if he were a failure," the commissaris said, "but it seemed he was a great success. His business did well, he was a wealthy man, he traveled a great deal, and he was only in his early thirties . . ."

"He was a silly man," the woman, whom the commissaris had in his notebook as Corin Kops, said.

"It's not so silly to be successful in business," the commissaris said. "For many people it is still the optimal goal."

"I didn't mean it in that way. I mean he was wasting his talents. He could have contributed something to society. Most people just live, like toadstools. They grow and after a while they begin to die. They are living objects, but Abe was much more than that."

"Yes," the commissaris said and, slumped back. "Quite. You said you and he discussed books. What sort of books did he like?"

She pursed her lips, as if she were going to whistle. Grijpstra looked at his watch. His stomach rumbled. "Peckish," Grijpstra thought. "I am feeling a bit peckish. I hope he'll take me to one of those bistros. I could do with a rare steak and baked potato. A large baked potato."

"Books without a moral. He read some travel books, written by adventurers. People who just roamed about and wrote down their thoughts. And he liked surrealist books."

"Surrealist?" Grijpstra stirred.

"It's a philosophy. Surrealist writers go deeper than the average novelist, by using dreams and unusual associations. They don't bother about surface logic or try to describe daily events but aim for the roots of human behavior."

"They do?" Grijpstra asked.

The commissaris brightened. "Like Nellie's bar, Grijpstra," he said and grinned. "Like what you think when you are fishing, or when you wake up in the morning."

"When I shave?" Grijpstra asked, and grinned too. "Lots of hot water and lather and a new razor blade and nobody in the bathroom and the door locked and swash, swash with the brush."

"What do you think about when you shave?" the commissaris asked. Grijpstra rubbed the short hairs on his skull energetically. "Hard to say, sir."

The woman showed interest. She was on her way to the kitchen, carrying the dirty coffee cups, but she stopped and turned.

"Try to describe your thoughts," Corin Kops said.

"About the sea," Grijpstra said. "Mostly about the sea, and I have never been a sailor, so that's strange, I suppose. But I think about the sea when I shave. Big waves and a blue sky."

"Could you give an example from Abe's life, miss?" the commissaris asked.

"Something surrealistic, you mean? But his whole life was like that. He lived a dream, even when he was being practical. He never gave expectable answers to sensible questions and he always seemed to be changing his mind. There was no set pattern in his life. The man was like a wet bar of soap."

She suddenly sounded exasperated. She looked at the commissaris in desperation. "Once he was here, at night, in the early hours of the morning. There was a gale on. The windows were rattling and I couldn't sleep. I saw him get up and told him to get back to bed. A hard wind always makes me nervous and I wanted him to be with me. But he said he was going sailing, and Louis Zilver told me later that the two of them took that small plastic yacht right out onto the big lake and they very nearly drowned."

She put down the tray. "The Germans killed his parents during the war, you know. Dragged them across the street and threw them into a cattle truck and gassed them. But he didn't seem to blame the Germans; he even took German as a second language at the university."

"The Germans must have meant to get him too," Grijpstra said.

"Yes, but the SS patrol missed him. He happened to be playing at a friend's house that morning. He didn't blame the Germans, he blamed the planets,"

"Planets?"

"Yes. He thought that the planets, Mercury and Neptune and especially Uranus—he was very interested in Uranus, and all the others, I forget their names—control our lives. If the planets form certain constellations there is war on earth, and when the constellations change again war stops and there is peace for a while. He had a very low opinion of human endeavor. He thought we are witless creatures, pushed into motion by forces entirely beyond our control. He often told me that there is nothing we can do about anything except perhaps to stop fighting fate and to try and move with it."

"But he was a very active person himself," the commissaris said.

"Exactly. I would say that to him too, but he only laughed and said his activity was due to Uranus, which happened to be very powerful at the time of his birth. Uranus is the planet of change."

"So he was hit by a cosmic ray when he was born and it made him the sort of person he was," the commissaris said. "I see."

"Made him jump about like a squirrel, eh?" Grijpstra asked.

She laughed. "More like an ape, a large hairy mad ape. An ape with strange gleaming eyes."

"Your friend must have been rather unreliable," the commissaris said.

She picked up the tray again but the commissaris' question seemed to sting her. "No. Not at all. He was trustworthy. He always paid his debts and kept his appointments. If he promised anything he would do it."

"Well, we've got to know him a little better," the commissaris said. "Thank you very much. We are ready now. All I would like to ask before we leave is if you remember where you were yesterday afternoon and last night."

She looked frightened. "You don't suspect *me* do you?"

"Not necessarily, but we'd like to know all the same."

"I was here, all afternoon and all evening. By myself. I was working on some examination papers."

"Did you see anyone? Speak to anyone? Did anyone phone you?"

"No."

"Would you have any idea who could have wanted to kill Abe Rogge?"

"No."

"Do you know *what* killed him?" Grijpstra asked.

"*What?* What do you mean?"

"Was it jealousy? Revenge? Greed?"

She shook her head.

"I am sorry," the commissaris said. "One more question has occurred to me. You have described your friend as a rather negative sort of superman. Never got upset, thought that nothing mattered, did everything well, sailed in storms and came back safely, read unusual books, and in French of all languages. Was he really that marvelous? No weaknesses at all?"

The woman's facial muscles, which had been working nervously, suddenly slacked.

"Yes," she said. "He had his weakness. He cried in

my arms once, and he cursed himself while he was shaving, here in my bathroom. He had left the door open and I could hear him."

"Why?"

"I asked him on both occasions and he gave the same answer. He said it was very close to him, so close that he could reach it, he thought, but then he couldn't."

"What?"

"He said he didn't know what it was."

They were almost at the door when Grijpstra, feeling that he hadn't been very helpful, tried again. "We met two of Mr. Rogge's friends, miss. Louis Zilver and Klaas Bezuur. Do you know how he was involved with them?"

She sighed. "He spent a lot of time with Louis. He even used to bring him here for dinner. Mr. Bezuur, I don't know very well. Abe used to talk about him. They were partners once, I think, but Bezuur has his own business now. Abe took me to Bezuur's factory one day, or his garage. I don't think they make the machinery over there; they just keep it around and rent it out, I think. Heavy trucks and all sorts of mobile machinery to make roads and move earth and so on. Abe was driving a bulldozer that afternoon, all over the yard. Louis was there too; he had a tractor. They were racing each other. Very spectacular. Later on Klaas joined them; he also drove a machine, with a big blade attached to it. He was rushing them, pretending to attack but he would reverse at the last moment. They frightened me."

"There was no bad feeling between Abe and Klaas?"

"No, apparently they had drifted apart but that was all. They were very affectionate when they met that afternoon. Embracing each other and shouting and calling each other names."

"When was that?"

"A few months ago, I think."

"Did he have any other close friends?"

She sighed again. "He knew thousands of people. Whenever we were in town together he seemed to be

greeting every other person. Girls he had slept with,
suppliers, customers, arty types, people he knew from
the street market or the university or boating trips. It
made me feel on edge, like I was escorting a TV star."

   "Probably annoyed them all at some time or other,"
Grijpstra said gloomily, holding the door open for the
commissaris. Corin was crying when he closed the door
behind him.

12

"Let's eat," the commissaris said.

"They always cry, don't they?" Grijpstra said. "Or they just look dumb, like animals, stupid animals. Toads, snails . . ." He was going to mention more stupid and slippery animals but the commissaris interrupted him.

"Snails," the commissaris said and leaned back into the foam rubber seat. "Yes, snails. I wouldn't mind having some snails for dinner. Constable!"

"Sir," the constable said.

"Do you remember that old windmill, the restaurant you took me to some time ago, with the public prosecutor?"

"Yes, sir."

"We'll go there again, that is, if the adjutant has nothing against eating snails."

Grijpstra looked dubious. "Never ate them before, sir."

"Oh, you'll like them. The French have been eating them for thousands of years and they are supposed to be more intelligent than we are. Did you say the lady struck you as stupid?"

"Not the lady in particular, sir. Most people behave stupidly when they connect with death."

"You aren't criticizing, you mean, you are observing."

Grijpstra looked hurt. "The police never criticize."

The commissaris reached out and patted Grijpstra's solid shoulder with his thin almost lifeless hand.

"Right, adjutant. You've remembered your lessons. We observe, connect, conclude and apprehend. If we can. The suspect always tries to get away, and when we do manage to catch him the lawyers will criticize and excuse him in turns and our observations will be made to fit in with whatever the lawyers say, and in the end nobody will really know what happened or why it happened." The commissaris' hand was back in his lap again. It suddenly became a fist and hit the seat.

"This is a silly case, Grijpstra. I don't understand how all these people link up. Take the lady we saw just now, for instance. Abe slept with her, but he slept with a number of women. What did he see in her? She isn't especially attractive either. Did you think she was attractive?"

Grijpstra's thick lips curled derisively and he shook his head. "No, sir. Thin legs, not a very good figure, a lot of fluffy curls on a round head. But there is no accounting for a man's taste."

"Her mind?" the commissaris asked, but Grijpstra's expression didn't change.

"A bookworm, sir."

"Right," the commissaris said. "Exactly. Living on her theories, or on what she thinks are her theories, on something other people and maybe a few books have droned into her. Surrealism indeed! And *that's* what the link between her and our corpse is supposed to be, a mutual interest in French surrealist novels."

"You don't believe in surrealism, sir?"

The commissaris shrugged and looked out of the window. The car was following the narrow road past the Amstel River and they had a clear view of a wide expanse of water, hardly ruffled by a quiet breeze which had lost most of its force in the river's protecting belt of reeds and bushes.

"Yes, yes," he said slowly, "but the word irritates me. No meaning. It's like saying 'God,' or the 'infinite' or 'the point where two parallel lines meet.' They'll say those words and wipe away a tear. What would a girl like Corin Kops, a brittle stale bunch of bones topped by an unspectacular brain, know about surrealism!"

Grijpstra looked away. He pretended to rub his mouth to hide his smile, remembering that he had once described the commissaris to de Gier as a dry stick topped by a razor blade.

"Hasn't understood anything at all," the commissaris continued. "She just doesn't know. They try to define something that can never be caught in a word, but they'll think of a word all the same and then use it as if it had real meaning. Like the Dutch Reformed preachers holding forth about God. In the old days anyway. They have learned a little more modesty now, and there aren't so many of them left, thank heaven. What do we know about reality? Maybe we do at moments. Like early this morning, with my half-witted turtle pottering about in the grass and a thrush singing away. Maybe I understood something then but it was gone when I tried to put my hand on it. But a woman like Miss Kops thinks she catches it and coins a word, and before you know it the word is in the dictionaries. Hey!"

Grijpstra, whose eyes had been closing, looked up.

"Constable!" the commissaris shouted. "Stop the car!"

The constable stood on the brakes and Grijpstra lurched forward.

"Back the car up," the commissaris said softly, "but slowly. Very slowly. We mustn't disturb him."

"There," the commissaris said. "See?"

Grijpstra saw the heron, a majestic specimen of its race, well over four feet high, standing under a willow on the right side of the road, its plume crowning the thin delicate head. A huge goldfish was held in its beak, tail and head hanging down.

The constable laughed. "He doesn't know what to do with it, sir. That fish must weigh a few pounds."

"That's right," Grijpstra said. "Herons catch small fish and swallow them. He'll never get that whopper through his throat. But how did he manage to catch a goldfish? There aren't any goldfish in the river and he's on the wrong side of the road anyway, the river is behind us."

"Must be a fishpond behind that mansion," the constable said. "The bugger sneaked in there and took his chance."

"Let's go," the commissaris said.

Grijpstra caught on five minutes later. The commissaris hadn't said anything and seemed half asleep, hands on knees, head reclining against the top of his seat.

"A heron is a lovely bird," Grijpstra said, "and that heron was a beauty."

"Indeed," the commissaris said.

"One doesn't often see a heron with a goldfish in his beak."

"Quite," the commissaris said.

Grijpstra tried once more. "I am glad you stopped the car, sir."

"Why?"

"The beauty of it, sir."

The commissaris waved at the river. "The river is beautiful too, Grijpstra, and it's there all the time. So are the trees, so is that old windmill over there. We are surrounded by beauty. Even the new blocks of apartments we saw this morning are beautiful, and not only at sunset or early in the morning."

"It's not the same," Grijpstra said.

"Yes. The heron was different. He had a goldfish in his beak. Most unusual. Maybe the sudden unlikely image shocked something free in you. It's only when we get shocked that we can see something, but it's tricky. Like a man suddenly being knocked down by a car.

He is crossing the street, dreaming away, and wham, there he is, flat on his back, with a wound somewhere or a broken bone. I've seen it dozens of times. They cry, they hold your hand, they are all upset. So they are rushed to the hospital and are shot full of dope, and whatever they were able to understand, because their world broke up, is drugged away again."

"That bird looked pretty stupid, sir," the constable at the wheel said gleefully.

"Like us," the commissaris said. "We've got a beautiful case, stuck right up our throat, but we are damned if we know what to do with it."

Dinner took an hour. They had half a dozen snails each and fresh toast and strong red wine from an unlabeled bottle. Grijpstra poked about suspiciously, extracting the small black rubbery lumps from their shells, frowning while he slowly chewed them.

"Well?" the commissaris asked.

"Very nice," Grijpstra said, carefully cleaning his plate with a piece of toast. "Good sauce this."

"More?"

Grijpstra thought. The commissaris nodded encouragingly.

"Yes."

Grijpstra ate another half dozen. He also ate half a chicken and a plateful of strawberries and asked the waiter for more whipped cream.

"If I can get it on your plate," the waiter said.

"Try."

The waiter ladled on more whipped cream.

"You can leave that pitcher on the table," the commissaris said, "and put it on the bill."

"You'd better not kiss your wife tonight," the commissaris said as they left the restaurant. "That sauce you liked so much was solid garlic."

"I never kiss my wife," Grijpstra said and burped. "Excuse me, sir."

"Never mind, but don't burp in the car. You'll knock out the driver and we still have to see that other girl."

Grijpstra nodded gravely but he wasn't listening. A second burp was forming itself at the bottom of his gullet and seemed stuck sideways, sideways and askew. It burned and cut simultaneously and he began to pat his chest anxiously in a vain attempt to dislodge the bubbly obstacle. The commissaris was still talking and the Citroën waited for them at the end of the path with the constable at the door.

"Funny fellow, don't you think?" the commissaris asked. "He always refuses to eat with me, poor chap still lives in the last century. He probably had a cup of coffee and fried eggs on toast on the terrace while we stuffed ourselves inside. I'll see if I can get his bill. Can't let him pay for himself, can I?"

Grijpstra was still patting his chest.

"What's wrong?"

"I'll be right back," Grijpstra said and turned off the path. Hidden behind a thicket of young ash trees he thumped his chest and wriggled his large body but the burp stayed where it was, obstinately lodged below an invisible impediment. Determined to free himself Grijpstra jumped up and down, flapping his arms and suddenly the burp, having grown meanwhile into a full-grown belch, roared out and touched his vocal cords, vibrating first into a growl and reaching the impact of a thunderclap at its summit.

Grijpstra dropped his arms and staggered back.

"Well done," the waiter said. He had been watching Grijpstra ever since he turned off the path.

"Beautiful," the waiter said now. "Never heard anything like it. I am surprised there are still leaves on the trees. Try a fart now. Go on."

Grijpstra felt too relieved to be hurt. "Shouldn't you be inside working?" he asked mildly.

"I should be," the waiter said, "but I am not. I am here, taking five minutes off and smoking a cigarette.

It's my last day at this establishment. I am starting a little snack bar in town next week."

"Where? Maybe I'll come and try it."

"Not you," the waiter said, threw down his cigarette, stamped on it, and walked away.

13

"WE ARE EARLY," the commissaris said to the constable. "You can drive about for half an hour if you like. There's a nature reserve close by. I've been there before, I even have a special pass. It isn't open to the public."

He fished around in his wallet and gave the pass to the driver. The constable turned it around and studied the little map on its reverse side.

"I can find it, sir. It shouldn't be more than a few kilometers from here."

Grijpstra was still exhausted and happy to let events take their course. The soft suspension of the car was lulling him to sleep and when he woke up because the commissaris touched his arm they were in the reserve. Once a graveyard, the place had lain untended for a hundred years or so; then the municipal authorities had discovered it again and promoted it into a special area, enlarging the land by buying the surrounding farms and a small estate, complete with the ruins of a castle and a moat leading into an artificial lake. The city had dipped into a wildlife fund for the money, and botanists and biologists now roamed the reserve, trying to find out what supposedly extinct flora and fauna they might run into.

"Untouched by filthy hands," the commissaris mumbled as he gazed at the landscape. The constable was driving slowly so that they could enjoy the sight of beeches and oaks grown to gigantic sizes, a glade, covered with the lush yellow of gorse, undergrowth bustling with rabbits and a lone pheasant standing on a rock. "Look," the commissaris said, and pointed at a spotted deer, watching them quietly from the cover of a broken gravestone.

"I could hit him easily from here," the constable said and touched the automatic pistol, resting in its holster under his blazer. "A perfect shot sir."

"You're joking," Grijpstra said grumpily.

"A policeman is a hunter," the commissaris said good-naturedly. "Don't scold the constable, adjutant. The thought occurred to me too."

He pointed his index finger at the buck. "Bam," the commissaris said. "You are dead. We'll have venison for dinner tomorrow."

The car was moving again. They were getting close to the lake and at a turn of the path they saw a flock of coots landing. The fat black little birds came in with their flat webbed feet spread, clumsily hitting the lake's still surface and splashing heavily before they flopped down, like puddings thrown in a comic movie.

"Ha," the constable said, but he wasn't laughing a minute later when the wide tires of the Citroën were crushing the first toads.

"What now?" the constable asked, and stopped the car, alarmed by the squashing noise which had suddenly burst on his eardrums. He got out and looked at the tarmac. Some ten flattened baby toads showed themselves on the hot tar of the path.

The commissaris and Grijpstra had got out too.

"You should have avoided them," Grijpstra said. "Toads are getting scarce nowadays."

"He couldn't have," the commissaris said. "He didn't see them, did you, constable?"

"No, sir. I heard them when they squashed. Bah. Horrible sound, wasn't it? Like popping balloons."

"There are lots of them," Grijpstra said.

The grass on both sides of the path was alive with toads. They were coming from the lake, and the car and the three men were in their way. The path became covered with their small slimy bodies and there seemed no way of avoiding their hopping progress. They were everywhere, crawling over the policemen's shoes, pushing against the car's tires. They could hear them too now, an oozing sound, as if thick wet sticky mud were being pumped through countless drainpipes.

"Let's get out of here," the commissaris said, shaking the animals off his shoes and inadvertently stepping on them.

The constable slipped and would have fallen if Grijpstra's heavy hand hadn't caught his elbow. They got back into the car.

"If we drive away I'll kill thousands of them," the constable said.

The commissaris looked at the lake. "They are still coming, they may be coming all day. This must be their hatching time. Perhaps there is a plague of toads. That damned gatekeeper shouldn't have let us in. Get us out of here, constable, we have an appointment to keep."

The toads crawled and sucked and squashed for hundreds of yards and the Citroën kept on crushing them. The constable was cursing, holding the wheel as if he wanted to wrench it out of its socket. The slime of the small corpses filled the grooves of the tires, forcing the car to slide crazily, and twice they slipped off the path with spinning wheels. Grijpstra felt sick and blocked his ears to drown the continuous slushing and squeezing. He was trying not to think of the snails, which he imagined sliding about in his stomach in a sea of whipped cream, and was breathing deeply. He could see the constable's wide staring eyes in the rearview mirror.

"That's it," the commissaris said cheerfully. "We are through. Go forward and reverse a couple of times on that sandy spot over there, it'll clean out the tires."

"That girl will be our last suspect for the time being," the commissaris was saying, "but Abe Rogge must have had a lot of close relationships. We are facing a crowd, Grijpstra. Maybe we haven't even started yet."

Grijpstra didn't answer and the commissaris leaned forward to get a closer look. Grijpstra's state of nerves didn't seem improved at all; if anything it seemed worse. The adjutant's skin looked gray and he wasn't able to control his hands, which were fidgeting with the end of his tie.

"Sir," the constable said, and pointed at a small freshly painted houseboat.

Grijpstra grunted and got out of the car. The commissaris wanted to follow but checked himself. Grijpstra was hopping about on one foot on the quay, yelling.

"Now what?" the commissaris asked.

"Careful, sir," Grijpstra shouted. "The pavement is full of shit."

The commissaris looked. It must have been a large dog, a large sick dog perhaps. The turds, of a greenish yellow color, covered several cobblestones and Grijpstra had stepped right in the middle. The constable closed his eyes, opened them again and forced his body to move. He walked around the car, opened the trunk and found a hard brush with a long handle. Grijpstra held on to a lamppost while the constable set to work.

"You *are* an excitable fellow," the commissaris said. "Haven't you ever stepped into dog turds before, adjutant?"

"Often," Grijpstra said irritably. "Every day of my life, I think. I attract dogshit. If there's one turd in a street I plow right through it. Some people think it's funny. I amuse them."

"I don't think it's funny," the commissaris said, "and neither does the constable."

"De Gier thinks it's funny. Yesterday, when we went to fetch the car in the police yard, I stepped into a turd and I was running so I slithered all over the pavement. He laughed, the bastard laughed! Tears in his eyes! Slapping his thighs! But dogshit is the same to me as a bleeding corpse to him. *I* don't laugh when he is leaning against walls and fainting and carrying on!"

"Hmm," the commissaris said, "but you are clean now. Thank you, constable. Let's get into that boat before anything else happens."

The girl was waiting for them in the doorway.

"Anything wrong?" she asked the adjutant. "Why were you jumping about?"

"Stepped in some dog droppings, miss."

"The German shepherd next door did that. He hasn't been feeling well lately. I meant to clean it up today but I forgot. Take your shoes off, my boat is all spick and span for once."

Grijpstra knelt down obediently. The commissaris slipped past him, found a comfortable-looking chair and sat down. The girl stayed with Grijpstra until both shoes, upside down, were placed in a corner near the door.

"Are you police officers?" the girl asked. "I always thought they wore raincoats and felt hats."

"You've been watching old movies," the commissaris said.

"Coffee?" the girl asked.

"No, thanks, miss."

The commissaris approved of the girl. Large lively eyes in a freckled face. Stiff pigtails with blue ribbons to keep them together. A dress, reaching her ankles, made out of gaily printed cotton. Irregular but very white teeth, a strong mouth. A ray of sunshine, the commissaris thought happily, just what we need to finish off a day's work.

"You've come about Abe?" the girl asked and looked

at Grijpstra, who was standing about forlornly. "Why don't you sit down?"

"Where?" Grijpstra asked.

"Right here." She pointed at a shapeless leather bag next to the commissaris' chair, got down on her haunches and thumped the bag. "It's quite comfortable, it's filled with pebbles. I bought it in Spain. Try it." Grijpstra sat down. "You see?"

"Yes, miss," Grijpstra said and screwed his wide bottom into the bag. Its back came up and supported his bulk; the pebbles were crunching inside.

"Yes," the commissaris said. "We've come about Abe. He was killed yesterday, as you know. We were told you were friendly with Mr. Rogge."

"Yes," the girl said. "Very friendly. We slept together."

"Yes, yes," the commissaris said.

"I like to be exact," the girl said brightly.

Why is she so damned cheerful? Grijpstra thought. The man is dead, isn't he? Can't she be upset? He moved and the pebbles crunched again.

"Don't look so worried. That bag won't break. Hundreds of people have sat on it."

"So Abe was your lover, eh?" he asked.

"He was my lover but I wasn't his mistress."

"I see," Grijpstra said doubtfully.

"I don't," the commissaris said. "If Mr. Rogge was your lover you were his mistress. Surely that's the right way of describing the relationship, isn't it?"

"No," the girl said, and smiled. "No, not at all. Abe slept with lots of girls; they came to him when he flicked his fingers—and wagged their tails. He didn't even have to seduce them, they just expected him to take his pants off and do the job. Not me. He came when *I* wanted him to come and he left me when *I* wanted him to leave and he had to talk to me and to listen to me. I never tried to fit into his schedule. I am a busy girl, I've got my own schedule. I study and the State is paying me to study; they gave me a nice grant.

I intend to finish my studies in time, ahead of time preferably. I don't play around."

It was a long speech and she delivered it almost vehemently, standing in the middle of the small room. Grijpstra was impressed. The commissaris appeared not to be listening. He had been looking around him. The interior of the boat looked as neat as its outside. She hadn't cluttered the room; everything which it contained seemed to fulfill a function. A large low table, stacked with books and paper and a typewriter. A few plants and a vase filled with freshly cut flowers.

He got up, and walked to the end of the room, stopping at a work bench. "Are you working on something, miss?"

"Tilda," the girl said, "Tilda van Andringa de Kempenaar. Just call me Tilda. That's a bird feeder, or, rather, it will be one day. I am having a little trouble with it."

"Van Andringa de Kempenaar," the commissaris said, and narrowed his eyes. The puckered forehead showed that he was thinking, trying to remember. "A noble name, it shows in our history books, doesn't it?"

"Yes," she said briskly, "a noble name, a noble family."

"I should address you as 'freule' perhaps."

"Not really," she said. "Tilda will do." She picked up her long dress, bent her knees and straightened up again. "We had estates once, and influence at court, and I don't think we paid taxes in those days, but my great-great-grandfather blew it all in Paris and ever since then we've been like the rest and worked for a living."

"I see," the commissaris said and bared his teeth mechanically. "A bird feeder, you said?"

"Yes. I like making things but this is more work than I anticipated. It still has to be covered with sheet metal and glass but I've got to get the inside right first. It's supposed to be ingenious you see. The bird has to sit on this little rod and then some feed will flow into that tray over there. There's a small trapdoor here connected to the rod. But it isn't working properly. There should be just enough feed going into the tray; I don't want to keep refilling the container. The whole thing will be hung outside when it's ready and the only way I can get at it will be via the roof. The windows on that side don't open."

"I see, I see," the commissaris said, replacing the structure. "Very clever. Did you design it yourself?"

"I had some help but not much. I like inventing. I was always making soap box carts when I was a child. One of them got a prize at school. I won a race in it. Want to see it?"

"Please," the commissaris and Grijpstra said.

She brought it in and went into a long technical explanation.

"Very clever," the commissaris said again.

"What do you study, Tilda?" Grijpstra asked.

"Medicine. I am in my third year. I want to be a surgeon."

"But you are still very young," Grijpstra said in an awed voice.

"Twenty-one."

"You'll have your degree in four years' time." Grijpstra was almost whispering. He couldn't imagine the girl as a graduate in medicine. He suddenly saw himself tied to a table in a white room. The girl was bending over him. She had a knife, the knife would cut into his skin, slicing a deep wound. Her fingers were touching exposed muscles, nerves, vital organs. A shiver touched the hairs on his neck.

"Nothing special," the girl said. She had seen Grijpstra's reaction and grinned wickedly. "Anybody who isn't downright stupid and who is willing to work hard for eight or ten hours a day can become a doctor."

"But you want to be a surgeon," Grijpstra said.

"Yes. I'll have to work in a hospital somewhere for another seven years or so. But it'll be worth it."

"Yes," the commissaris said. "Do you have any idea who killed your friend, Tilda?"

The grin froze on her face. She suddenly seemed to become aware of herself, standing halfway between her interrogators. "No. No, I have no idea. He was always so happy and full of life. I am sure nobody disliked him. Esther said that he was killed in some mysterious way? Is that right?"

"That's right," the commissaris said. "You wouldn't have any photographs, would you? We only saw him dead."

Her eyes were moist now. "Yes, holiday snapshots. I'll get them."

They looked at the album. Abe Rogge at the helm of his boat, and running in the surf, and leaning over the railing of a ferry, and at the wheel of an antique motorcar. Louis Zilver was in some of the photographs, and Tilda herself, looking healthy and attractive.

"Fishing," the commissaris said. "Did he fish a lot?" He pointed at a photo showing Abe struggling with a fishing rod, bent backward, pulling with all his might.

"That was in North Africa," the girl said, "last year. Just the two of us went. He had some gamefish on the hook, took him all afternoon to bring it in. It was such a lovely fish that I made him throw it back. It must have weighed a hundred kilos."

"Where were you yesterday afternoon and last night?" Grijpstra asked.

"Here."

"Anyone with you?"

"No, several people knocked on the door and the telephone rang but I didn't answer. I am working on a test. I should be working at it now too. They didn't give me much time and it's an important credit."

"Yes," the commissaris said. "We must be going."

"Hard-boiled little thing," Grijpstra said in the car. "It won't be easy to shake her. She almost broke down when you asked her to show the photographs but that was the only time she weakened. I bet she is the local chairman of some red women's organization."

"Yes, and a proper freule too," the commissaris said. "I think one of her ancestors was a general who fought Napoleon. I forget what he did now but it was something brave and original. She'll be a good surgeon. Maybe she'll invent a way to cut hemorrhoids painlessly."

Grijpstra looked up. "Do you have hemorrhoids, sir?"

"Not anymore, but it hurt when they took them out. Did you see that bird feeder?"

"Yes, sir. A well-designed construction. Do you think she could manufacture a deadly weapon, sir? Something which can shoot a spiked ball?"

"I am sure she can," the commissaris said. "It would work with a powerful spring. I counted six springs in her bird thing."

"It's a thought," Grijpstra said, "but that's all it is. Whatever she had going with Rogge must have been going well, so why would she go to a lot of trouble to kill him?"

"The female mind," the commissaris said. "A great mystery. My wife went to a lot of trouble because she didn't like the man who delivered oil for our central heating. She phoned his boss and said that if they couldn't send someone else she would close the account. I was never able to find out what she had against the man; he seemed a pleasant rather witless fellow to me. But now we are buying oil from some other company. And my wife hardly ever gets upset. This girl would fly into a rage at the slightest provocation. Made that great hulking fellow throw back a fish he had fought with for hours. Made you take off your shoes. Knows exactly what she wants. Studies like mad. Builds involved gadgets just for fun. Has her sex life arranged all *her* way."

"A nasty bundle of energy," Grijpstra said. "Perhaps we should go back tomorrow, sir, take her to the morgue and confront her with the corpse. Interrogate her for a few hours. She has no alibi, she could easily have sneaked out to the Rogge house. She is a small girl. The riot police would have let her through. Maybe she was carrying a parcel containing the device that shot the ball. She climbed onto the roof of that old ship lying opposite the house, called Abe . . ."

"Could be," the commissaris said, "but I am taking you home now. We'll see tomorrow. Maybe de Gier and Cardozo will pick up a clue at the street market. You and I can sit and think for a day, or you can go out to the market too."

The car stopped in front of Grijpstra's house. The constable looked back as he drove away.

"He isn't going home, sir," the constable said. "He hesitated at the door and walked away."

"Really?" the commissaris asked.

"Well, he's right, I think," the constable said. "Some wife the adjutant has. Did you see that woman popping her head out of the window this morning, sir?"

"I did," the commissaris said.

14

WHEN DE GIER turned the key he could hear Oliver's nails scratching the inside of the door. He also heard the telephone.

"It never stops," he said to Esther, stepping aside so that she could enter first, and bending down. Oliver ran straight into his hand, pressed low to the floor, intent on escape. "Here," de Gier said and caught him. "Don't run away, there's nothing outside there. Just a lot of fast cars and a hot street. Here! And don't scratch."

The telephone was still ringing. "Yes, yes, yes," de Gier said, and picked it up. Esther had taken the cat out of his arms and was nuzzling it, whispering into its ear. Oliver closed his eyes, went limp and purred. The nails slid back and his paws became soft playthings of fur. He pushed a paw against her nose, and kept it there.

"That's nice," de Gier said. "I have never seen him do that to anyone except myself. Silly cat loves you."

"Is it silly to love me?" Esther asked, and before he

had time to think of an answer, "Who was that on the
telephone? You look all grumpy."

"The commissaris."

"I thought he was a very pleasant man."

"He is not," de Gier said, "and he shouldn't phone
me. He is fussing. Did I get the schedule for tomorrow
organized? Did I speak to Cardozo about it? Did I do
this? Did I do that? Of course I did it all. I always do
everything he tells me. Why doesn't he fuss with Grijpstra? But he had Grijpstra with him all day, they had
dinner together, while I was sent on an inane errand."

"What errand?"

"Never mind," de Gier said. "Take your coat off
and I'll make tea. Or I can open a can of shrimp soup,
I have had it in the fridge for ages, waiting for the right
occasion. We can have a drop of Madeira in it and eat
some hot buttered toast and a salad. And we can look
at the geraniums while we eat. The one in the middle is
doing very well. I've been feeding it expensive drops
and it is responding. See?"

"You like your balcony, don't you?"

"It's better than a garden. I don't have to wear myself out in it. I am growing some cabbage seed now, in
that pot in the corner. The little boy in the flat upstairs
gave me the seeds and they came up in a few weeks,
just as he said. They are in flower too now. I used to
study the buds through a magnifying glass; I could almost see them swell."

"I thought you would be more interested in fingerprints."

"No," de Gier said. "Fingerprints don't grow, they
are just there, left by a fool who didn't mind what he
was doing. We hardly ever find fingerprints anyway
and if we find them they belong to a sweet innocent."

She was helping him in the kitchen and sent him
out, once she knew where everything was. He sat down
on his bed and talked to her through the open door.
She didn't take long and served the meal on a detach-
able board, which he pulled from the wall and which

came down to about a foot from the bed's surface, suspended by hinges on one side and a chain on the other.

"Very ingenious," she said. "This is a very small
apartment but it looks quite spacious somehow."

"Because I have no furniture," he said. "Just the bed,
and the chair in the other room. I don't really like
having people here, they make the place overflow.
Grijpstra is O.K., he doesn't move. And you, of course.
It's marvelous having you here."

She leaned over and kissed his cheek. The telephone
rang again.

"It never stops," de Gier said. "It. The whole thing.
It's still moving and I want to be out of it. There should
be a way of dropping out of activity. Smashing the telephone would be a good start."

"Answer it," she said, "and then come back to me.
And to the toast, it's still hot."

"Cardozo?" de Gier asked.

"Yes," Cardozo said, "your faithful assistant is reporting. I am about to start organizing the truck and the
merchandise and the permit for the street market and
everything, but I thought I'd better run through all the
details with you once more before I started."

De Gier sighed. "Cardozo?"

"Yes."

"Cardozo, it's all yours. I want you to prove yourself. Get the whole rigmarole going, Cardozo. Do more
than we are asking you to do. Find out what the textiles
are worth. We have to sell them at the right price tomorrow. We can't give state property away, can we?"

"No," Cardozo said.

"Right. Besides we don't want the other hawkers to
be suspicious. We have to be just right. Think about this
business. Try and *become* a hawker. Think yourself
into it. Get the thought into your subconscious. Try and
dream about it tonight."

"What are *you* going to do?" Cardozo asked.

"I am going to be here, right here in my flat and
think with you. Don't feel alone, I am with you, right
behind you, Cardozo. Every step of the way."

"When I am carrying those heavy bales out of the police store?"

"Yes."

"Heaving them into the van?"

"Yes."

"That'll be nice."

"Yes. And if there's any problem you can't solve—I don't think there will be any, for you are competent and well trained and an asset to the force—then grab the nearest telephone and dial my number. I'll advise you."

"About how to carry those heavy bales into the van?"

"Yes. Take a deep breath before you lift them. Then stop your breath while you move your arms. Get your shoulder and stomach muscles to help. Heave-ho! You'll find it easy if you go about it the right way."

"I am glad you have faith in me," Cardozo said. "Maybe I will tell the commissaris about your faith in me, sometime when I happen to run into him and we'll be chatting about this and that."

"Oh, no, you won't," de Gier said. "I read the report in your file. The character report. You were picked for the murder squad because you have all the right qualities. Initiative for instance. And an inquisitive and secretive mind. And you are ambitious. You can be trusted to react properly when in a difficult spot. And you are reliable. Did you know all those things about yourself?"

"No," Cardozo said, "and I don't believe that report. It must have been made up by the psychologist who interviewed me. A rat-faced long-haired nervous wreck. I thought he was a suspect when I met him and I was watching him very carefully."

"Psychology is a new science, a long-haired rat-faced science. They all look like that. They have to, or they are no good. And please stop arguing, Cardozo. Haven't you learned by now that nothing is gained by arguing?"

"Yes, sergeant," Cardozo said. "Sorry, sergeant. Forgot myself a moment, sergeant. Won't happen again, sergeant. Do you want me to report when I've got it all arranged, sergeant?"

"No," de Gier said. "That won't be necessary. I'll see you tomorrow morning, at the police garage at eight-thirty sharp. Good luck."

He put down the telephone and went back to the bed.

"Excellent young man," he said to Esther, "and clever too."

"Aren't you clever?"

"No," de Gier said.

"Are you a good detective?"

"No."

"Do you try to be?"

"Yes."

"Why?" He laughed, leaned over and kissed her.

"No. I want to know. Why do you try to be a good detective?"

He kissed her again. He said something about her hair and how well the kimono looked on her and how glad he was that she had changed her clothes while he was talking on the telephone. And how slender her body was.

"Yes," she said. "You are a charmer. But why do you try to be a good detective?"

"To please the commissaris," he said, trying to make the remark pass off as a joke.

"Yes," Esther said seriously. "I had a professor once I wanted to please. He seemed a very advanced little old man to me, and I loved him because he was so ugly and because he had such a big bald head. His mind was very quick but it was also deep, and I was sure he knew things that I should know. He was a strangely happy man and yet I knew that he had lost everything he cherished during the war and lived by himself in an old, untidy and very depressing house. I did very well in his class although his subject hardly interested me when I began. He taught medieval French and he made it come alive again."

"Crime interests me," de Gier said. "It interested me before I began to work under the commissaris."

"Why?" He lay back, stretching out an amorous arm which she didn't resist. "Why do you like crime?"

"I didn't say I liked crime, I said it interested me. Crime is sometimes a single mistake, more often a series of mistakes. I try to understand why criminals make mistakes."

"Why? To catch them?"

"I am not a hunter," de Gier said. "I hunt, because it is part of my work but I don't really enjoy it."

"So what are you?"

He sat up, looking for his pack of cigarettes. She gave him the pack and flicked her lighter. Her kimono opened and she adjusted it.

"Must we talk?" de Gier said. "I can think of better things to do."

She laughed. "Yes. Let's talk for a little while, I'll shut up in a minute."

"I don't know what I am," de Gier said, "but I am trying to find out. Criminals are also trying to find out what they are. It's a game we share with them."

His voice had gone up and Oliver woke and yowled.

"Oliver!" Esther said.

The cat turned its head and looked at her. He made a series of sounds, low sounds in the back of his throat, and stretched, putting a forepaw on her thigh.

"Go and catch a bird," de Gier said, as he picked him up and put him on the balcony, closing the door after him.

"Don't be jealous," Esther said.

"I *am* jealous," de Gier said.

"Don't you have any idea what you are?"

"Yes," he said and lay down on the bed, pulling her down, "a vague idea. A feeling rather. But it will have to become a lot clearer."

"And you became a policeman to find out?"

"No. I happened to become a policeman. I wasn't planning anything when I left school. I have an uncle in the police and he mentioned the possibility to my father and before I knew what I was doing I had signed a form and was answering questions and saying 'yes' to all of them and then suddenly I was in uniform, with a stripe on my arm, and eight hours a day of classes."

"My brother also wanted to find out what he was," Esther said. "It's dangerous to be like that. You'll get yourself killed."

"I don't think I would mind," de Gier said and tugged at her kimono.

They fell asleep afterward and de Gier woke up an hour later because Oliver was throwing his body against the glass balcony door, making it rattle. He got up and fed the cat, cutting the meat carefully into thin slices. He lay down again, without disturbing Esther, who lay on her side, gently breathing. Her breathing excited him again. He turned over and looked at the geraniums and forced his mind to concentrate. He wanted to think about the spiked ball, the ball which had smashed the life out of Esther's powerful brother. He knew this was the best time to think, when his body was almost all asleep, leaving his brain to function on its own. It had made him conclude, early that morning, that the ball had been connected to a line, probably an elastic line. He had remembered some little boys playing ball on the balcony of a hotel in France. He had been watching them from the lounge, several years ago now, during a holiday shared with a police secretary, who had turned out to be very high-strung and possessive and who had changed the promised pleasure of the trip into a series of fights and withdrawals. He had been trying to get away from her that day and had been on his way out through the lounge when he saw the kids. They had a ball attached to some heavy weight and they were hitting it with miniature bats. They couldn't lose the ball for it could only travel a certain length. He hadn't been trying to think of kids playing, he had only concentrated on the mystery of the spiked ball and the picture of the kids and their gadget had suddenly popped up.

The ball had been thrown or shot into Abe's room but it hadn't stayed there. He was sure that the killer had never been in the room. If he had, there would have been a fight. Esther and Louis Zilver were in the house at the time. They would have heard the fight. There would have been shouts, furniture would have been pushed around, bodies would have struggled and fallen. The killer would have had to leave the house after Abe's death. He would have had to take the risk that either Esther or Louis would see him. De Gier was sure that the murder had been planned. Planned with a hellish machine. He had seen an exhibition of hellish machines at the police museum. Fountain pens that spout poison, rings with hidden steel thorns moved by a spring, very involved machines that will trigger off an explosion, trapdoors, heavy weights that will fall at the right moment. But not a spiked ball that disappears after it has done its work. And yet he knew that he knew the answer. He had seen something once, something that was capable of moving a spiked ball. Where had he seen it?

It would have to be something ordinary, innocuous. Something the riot policemen could see without having second thoughts. And it had to be noiseless. A bang would have alarmed the constables who were uneasy anyway that day. Something the killer could carry through the Straight Tree Ditch and smile at the constables as he carried it.

His eyes were closing. He struggled. The answer was close; all he had to do was grab it.

He fell asleep and woke up two hours later. Esther wasn't on the bed. He heard her in the kitchen. She was stirring something in a pot. The smell reached him, a good smell which touched his stomach. A stew. She must have found the minced meat and the fresh vegetables. He got up and stuck his head into the small kitchen. She had some rice at the boil too.

They ate, and listened to records. De Gier felt happy, unbelievably and completely happy. He also felt guilty and he opened a can of sardines for Oliver.

15

THE ALBERT CUYP is a long narrow street cutting through one of Amsterdam's uglier parts, where houses are thin high slabs of bricks pushed together in endless rows, where trees won't grow and where traffic is eternally congested. The street market is the heart of an area consisting of stone and tar, and its splash of color and sound feeds some life into what otherwise wouldn't be much other than a hell of boredom, in which the human ant lives out its sixty or seventy years of getting up and going to bed, being busy in between with factory and office work, and TV programs and a bit of drinking at the corner bar. It was an area that both de Gier and Cardozo knew well, for it breeds crime, mostly sad and always nonspectacular. The neighborhood is known for its family fights, drug pushing in a small way, burglaries and a bit of robbery, committed by youth gangs who swagger about, waylaying the elderly passerby, stealing cars and motorized bicycles, and molesting lonely homosexuals. The area is doomed, for city planning will do away with it, blow it up with dynamite to make room for blocks of apartments set in parks, but the city works slowly and the street market will be there for many years to come, functioning as a gigantic department store, selling food and household goods cheaply, providing an outlet for the national industry's unsalable goods and for adventurer-merchants who import for their own account, or smuggle, or, rarely, buy stolen goods.

Cardozo had managed to force the gray van on to the sidewalk and was unloading bale after bale of gaily printed textiles, which de Gier stacked on the worn planks of a corner stall, assigned to them for the day by the market master, who had given them a knowing wink when de Gier, waving his license, looked him up in his little office.

"Good luck," the market master said. "You'll be after Rogge's killer, I bet. You'd better get him. Abe Rogge was a popular man here and he'll be missed."

"Don't tell anyone," de Gier said.

The market master was shaking his head energetically.

"I don't tell on the police. I need the police here. I wish you would patrol the market more regularly. Two uniformed constables can't cover a mile of market."

"There are plainclothes police as well."

"Yes," the market master said, "but not enough. There's always a bit of trouble here, especially on a hot day like this. We need more uniforms. If they see a shiny cap and nicely polished buttons they quiet down quickly. I have been writing to the chief constable's office. He always answers, but it's the same answer. Short of staff."

"Complain, complain, complain!" de Gier said.

"What do you mean?"

"What I say. Go on complaining. It helps. You'll get more constables."

"But they'll come from some other part of town and there'll be trouble down *there*."

"So someone else can start complaining."

"Yes," the market master said, and laughed. "I am

only concerned about my own troubles. What about you? Will you catch your man?"

"Sure," de Gier said, and left.

But he wasn't so sure when he got back to the stall. Cardozo was complaining too. The bales were too heavy.

"I'll get you some coffee," de Gier said.

"I can get my own coffee. I want you to help me unload these bales."

"Sugar and milk?"

"Yes. But help me first."

"No," de Gier said and left the stall. He found a girl carrying a tray with empty glasses, who took his order. He ordered meat rolls too and hot dogs.

"You are new, aren't you?" The girl was pretty and de Gier smiled at her.

"Yes. First day here. We've been on other markets, never down here."

"Best market in the country. What do you sell?"

"Lovely fabrics for dressmaking and curtains."

"Will you give me a special price?" The girl reached out with her free hand and patted his cheek.

"Sure." He smiled again and she swung her hip at him in response. He wasn't in a hurry to get back to the stall, but Cardozo saw him and shouted and jumped up and down, waving his arms.

Together they finished the stall, draping some of the textiles in what they thought to be an attractive display.

"This is no good," Cardozo muttered as he worked. "That fellow on the other side of the street knows who we are. He keeps on looking at us. Who is he anyway?"

De Gier looked and waved. "Louis Zilver. I asked the market master to give us a place close to him. He was Abe Rogge's partner. He's selling beads and wool and embroidery silk and all that sort of thing."

"But if he knows us he'll spread the news, won't he?"

"No, he won't, why should he?"

"Why shouldn't he?"

"Because he is the dead man's friend."

"He may be the dead man's killer."

De Gier sipped his coffee and stared at Cardozo, who was glaring at him from between two bales of cloth. "What are you so excited about? If he is the killer we are wasting our time here for we'll have to get at him in some other way. But if he isn't he'll protect us. He knows he is a suspect and if we find the killer he'll be cleared; besides, he may really want us to catch the murderer. He's supposed to be Rogge's friend, isn't he? There is such a thing as friendship."

Cardozo snorted.

"Don't you believe in friendship?"

Cardozo didn't answer.

"Don't you?"

"I am a Jew," Cardozo said, "and Jews believe in friendship because they wouldn't have survived without it."

"That isn't what I mean."

"What do you mean?"

"Friendship," de Gier said. "You know, love. One man loves another. He is glad when the other man is glad and sad when the other man is sad. He identifies with the other man. They are together, and together they are more than two individuals added up."

"You don't have to spell it out for me," Cardozo said. "I won't believe you anyway. There's such a thing as a shared interest and the idea that two men can do more than one. I can understand that but I won't go for love. I have been in the police for some time now. The friends we catch always rat on each other after a while."

"Love your neighbor," de Gier said.

"Are you religious?"

"No."

"So why preach at me?"

De Gier touched Cardozo's shoulder gingerly. "I am not preaching at you. Love your neighbor; it makes sense, doesn't it? Even if it happens to be a religious command."

"But we don't love our neighbors," Cardozo said, furiously pushing at a bale of lining which had fallen over. "We are envious of our neighbors, we try to grab things from them, we annoy them. And we make fun of them if we can get away with it and we kill them too if they don't want to put up with our demands. You can't prove history wrong. I was too young to have been in the last war but I've seen the documentaries, and I've heard the stories and seen the numbers burned into people's arms. We have an army to make sure that the neighbors across the frontier behave themselves and we have a police force to make sure that we behave ourselves within the frontiers. You know what the place would be like if the police didn't patrol it?"

"Stop kicking that bale," de Gier said. "You are spoiling the merchandise."

"Without the police society would be a mad shambles, sergeant, a free fight for all. I am sure that Zilver fellow doesn't care two hoots if we catch the killer or not, and if he does care he has a personal interest."

"Revenge, for instance," de Gier said.

"Revenge is selfish too," Çardozo said, "but I was thinking of money. He'll want us to make an arrest if he can profit by the arrest."

"You've been drinking with Grijpstra," de Gier said, and helped to lift the bale.

"No. *You* have. Last night."

De Gier looked hurt. "Last night, dear friend, I was at home. I only spent a few minutes with Grijpstra at Nellie's bar and half that time went on a telephone call. He didn't want me around so I left. Nellie didn't want me around either."

"Nellie?" Cardozo asked.

De Gier explained.

"Boy!" Cardozo said. "As big as that? Boy!"

"As big as that," de Gier said, "and Grijpstra wanted them all to himself. So I left. I checked out two prostitutes who were supposed to be Bezuur's alibi and after that I went home."

"Bezuur?" Cardozo asked. "Who is he? I am supposed to help you and the adjutant but nobody tells me anything. Who is Bezuur?"

"A friend of Abe Rogge."

Cardozo asked more questions and de Gier explained.

"I see," Cardozo said. "What about the callgirls? Had they been with him all night?"

"So they said."

"Did you believe them?"

"According to Grijpstra there were six empty champagne bottles lying about in Bezuur's bungalow, and there were cigarette burns on the furniture and stains on the walls. An orgy. Who remembers what happens during an orgy? Maybe they were out on the floor half the night."

"Did they look as if they had been?"

"They looked O.K." de Gier said. "One of them even looked pretty nice. But they had had time for their beauty sleep and they knew I was coming. I didn't know the address so I couldn't jump them."

"Couldn't you have checked with the telephone company?"

"I could have but it would have been difficult. It was Sunday, remember? And maybe I was too lazy to try and jump them."

"So what did you do afterward?"

"I went home and I went to bed. And in between I was weeding the flower boxes on my balcony. And I had a late supper with my cat."

Cardozo smiled. "You are a lucky man, sergeant."

"Don't call me sergeant. Why am I lucky?"

Cardozo shrugged. "I don't know. You are older than I am but you are like a child sometimes. You enjoy yourself, don't you? You and that silly cat."

"He isn't a silly cat. And he loves me."

"There we go again," Cardozo said and began to tug at another bale. "Love. I saw a poster in a bookshop last week. A love poster. Half-naked girls with frizzy hair sitting under a beautiful tree chanting away while birds fly around and angels gaze down. It's a craze. When I was still in uniform we had one of these love places a block away from the station. We had complaints every night. The girls would have their bags stolen and the boys had their wallets rolled and they were buying hash which turned out to be caked rub- bish and they had knives pulled on them and they got the clap and crabs and the itch. I've been in there dozens of times and it was the same thing every night, dirty and smoky and silly and hazy. Some of them would catch on and drift away, but there were always others who hadn't learned yet and who were begging to get in."

"The wrong place," de Gier said. "Brothels are the wrong place too. And Nellie's bar unless your name is Grijpstra and Nellie falls for you. But love exists." He patted his pockets.

"Cigarette?" Cardozo asked, and offered his tobacco pouch and packet of cigarette papers.

"Thanks," de Gier said. "You see, you are giving me something I haven't asked for. So you care for my well-being."

"So I love you," Cardozo said. De Gier felt embar- rassed and Cardozo grinned.

"I only offered you a cigarette because I know that I won't have any cigarettes sometime and I will want you to give me one. It's an investment for the future."

"And if I was dying?" de Gier asked. "Say I was going to be shot in five minutes' time and I asked you for a cigarette. Would you give me one? I would never be in a position to return the gift, would I?"

Cardozo thought.

"Well?"

"Yes, I would give you a cigarette, but I am sure I would have some selfish reason, although I can't think of the reason now."

"How much?" a voice asked. An old lady had come to the stall and was fingering a piece of cloth.

"Twelve guilders a meter, darling," Cardozo said, "and ten percent off if you buy five meters. That's lovely curtain material. It'll brighten up your room and it's guaranteed not to fade."

"Expensive," the old lady said.

"What do you mean, dear? It's two meters wide.

They'll charge you three times as much in any store, and it won't be as nice as this. This came from Sweden and the Swedish designers are the best in the world. Look at those flowers. Fuchsias. You'll be sitting in your room and you'll draw the curtains and the light will filter through the material and you'll be able to see the nice red flowers. Aren't they pretty? See, every petal is printed beautifully."

"Yes," the old lady said dreamily.

"Take five yards, dear, ten guilders a yard."

"I haven't got fifty guilders on me."

"How much have you got?"

"Thirty, and I only need three yards."

"For you I will do everything, darling. Give me the scissors, mate."

But he didn't start cutting until the lady had counted out her thirty guilders.

"I thought you said we should get eight guilders for that cloth," de Gier said.

"Start high, you can always come down. And she's got a bargain anyway."

"I wouldn't have that material in my flat if you paid me."

"Stop fussing," Cardozo said. "She selected the cloth herself, didn't she? And it's first-class material, confiscated from a first-class smuggler who tried to bring it in without paying duty and sales tax."

Other customers came and bought. Cardozo was yelling and waving and de Gier handled the scissors. After a while de Gier was selling too, joking and flirting with an odd assortment of females.

"Maybe we should do this for a living," he said during a short pause. A juggler on a collection of soap boxes was attracting everybody's attention and they had time to breathe.

"We have made more than we would normally make in a week working as policemen," Cardozo admitted, "but we have the right goods. It takes time and money to find this type of merchandise."

"I am sure we could do it."

"Yes, we'll find the right goods and we might get rich. A lot of these hawkers are rich. Abe Rogge was rich, or so you told me anyway. You want to get rich, de Gier?"

"Perhaps."

"You would have to leave the police."

"I wouldn't mind."

"Right," Cardozo said, trying to smooth down a piece of machine-made lace. "I'll join you if you want to become a merchant, but I don't think you ever will. I think you were born to become a policeman, like me. Maybe it's a vocation."

The juggler came to collect. He had drawn a lot of people to their corner of the market. Cardozo gave him some coins.

"Thanks," de Gier said. The juggler, an old man with a sun-tanned bald head smiled, showing a messy array of broken brown teeth.

"Thanks for nothing, buddy," the juggler said. "I'll be performing a hundred yards down now and drawing the crowd away from you again, but maybe I'll put them in a good mood and they'll be free with their money. You'd better hurry up though; we'll have rain in a minute and they'll melt away like whores who have seen the patrol car."

"Did you hear that?" de Gier asked. "He mentioned the police. Do you think he knows about us?"

"Maybe."

"Maybe not," de Gier said, and looked at the sky. It had become very hot and sweat prickled under his shirt. The clouds were lead-colored and low. The street sellers were putting up sheets of transparent plastic and pulling in their goods.

The clouds burst suddenly and cold heavy rain drowned the market, catching women and small children in midstreet, forcing them to scatter for cover. Sheets of water blocked de Gier's view and roared down, splashing up again from the pavement over his feet and trouser legs, dribbling down from the canvas roof and hitting him in the neck. Cardozo was shouting something and pointing at the stall next to them, but de Gier couldn't make out the words. He vaguely saw the old hawker and his wife scrambling about, but couldn't work out what was expected of him until Cardozo pulled him over and handed him a carton of vegetables and pointed at a VW bus parked on the sidewalk. Together they filled the small bus with their neighbor's merchandise, which the old man had stored under his stall and which was now in danger of being swept down the street by the torrent. De Gier was wet through and cursing but there seemed no end to the potatoes, cucumbers, baby squashes, bananas and cabbages.

"Thanks, mate," the old man and his wife kept on saying. De Gier muttered in reply. Cardozo was grinning like a monkey.

"Lovely to see you working for a change," Cardozo screamed right into de Gier's ear, so that it needed rubbing to make it function again.

"Don't shout," he shouted and Cardozo grinned again, his sharp face alight with devilish mirth.

The rain stopped when they had filled the bus and the sun was back suddenly, brightening a dismal scene of floating cartons and cases and sodden merchants splashing around their stalls mumbling and cursing, and shaking themselves like dogs climbing out of a canal.

"Hell," de Gier said, trying to dry his hair and face with a crumpled handkerchief. "Why did we have to help those fools? They could see the rain was coming, couldn't they?"

"Friendship," Cardozo said, rubbing his hands and waving at the coffee girl, who came staggering toward them carrying her tray filled with glasses of hot coffee and a dish of meat rolls and sausages smeared with mustard. "Love your neighbor, I remembered. There's nothing those old people can ever do to repay us, is there?"

De Gier smiled in spite of his discomfort. Cold drops were running down his back, touching his buttocks, the only dry part of his body. "Yes," he said, and nodded. "Thanks."

"Thanks for what?" Cardozo asked, suddenly cautious.

"For the lesson, I like to learn."

Cardozo studied de Gier's face. De Gier's smile seemed genuine. Cardozo sipped his coffee, shoving his tobacco and paper toward the sergeant, who immediately rolled two cigarettes, placing one between Cardozo's lips. He struck a match.

"No," Cardozo said. "I don't trust you, sergeant."

"What *are* you talking about?" de Gier asked pleasantly.

"Ah, there you are," Grijpstra said. "Loafing about as I expected. I thought you were supposed to be street sellers. Shouldn't you be trying to sell something? If you hang about in the back of your stall drinking coffee and exchanging the news of the day, you'll never get anywhere."

"Cardozo," de Gier said. "Get the adjutant a nice glass of coffee and a couple of sausages."

"Don't call me adjutant down here, de Gier, and I'll have three sausages, Cardozo."

"That'll be five guilders," Cardozo said.

"That'll be nothing, take it out of the till. You must have collected some money this morning while we were running around catching Turks."

"Turks?" de Gier and Cardozo asked in one voice.

"Turks, two of them, shot them both and took them to the hospital. I hope the one fellow won't die. He got a bullet through the left lung."

"Run along, Cardozo," de Gier said. "What's with the Turks, Grijpstra?"

Grijpstra sat down on a bale of cloth and lit a small cigar. "Yes. Turks. Silly fools held up a bank using toy pistols, beautiful toys, indistinguishable from the real thing. The one had a Luger and the other a big army-model Browning, made of plastic. The bank has an alarm and they managed to push the button. A sixteen-year-old girl pushed it while she was smiling at the robbers. The manager was too busy filling his pants. I happened to be at a station close by and got there on foot, as the

patrol cars arrived. The fools threatened us with their
toys and they got shot, one in the leg, the other in the
chest. It was over in two minutes."

"Did you shoot them?" de Gier asked.

"No. I had my gun out but I didn't even have time
to load. The constables fired as soon as they arrived."

"They shouldn't have."

"No, but they lost a man some months ago, remember? He stopped a stolen car and got shot dead before
he could open his mouth. These were the dead man's
friends. They remembered. And the toys looked real
enough."

"I thought those toys weren't sold anymore in the
shops?"

"The Turks bought them in England," Grijpstra said,
and shrugged. "Some happy shopkeeper made a few
shillings in London and now we have two bleeding
Turks in Amsterdam."

Cardozo came back and offered a plate of sausages.
Grijpstra's hand shot out and grabbed the fattest sau-
sage, stuffing it into his mouth in one movement.

"Vrgrmpf," Grijpstra said.

"They are hot," Cardozo said. "I would have told
you if you had waited one second."

"Rashf," Grijpstra said.

"Has he come to help us, de Gier?"

"Ask him when he has finished burning his mouth."

Grijpstra was nodding.

"He has come to help us, Cardozo."

"Are you selling this stuff or are you just showing it?"
an old woman with a face like a hatchet was asking.

"We are selling it, dearest," de Gier said, and came
forward.

"I am not your dearest, and I don't like that lace
much. Haven't you got any better?"

"It's handmade in Belgium, lady, handmade by farm
women who have done nothing but lace-making since
they were four years old. Look at the detail, see here."

De Gier unrolled the bale, holding the material up.

"Nonsense," the old woman said. "Rubbish, that's machine-made. How much is it anyway?"

De Gier was going to tell her the price when the wind caught the underpart of their canvas roof and pushed it straight up. Several bucketloads of ice-cold water shot off the top, and all of it hit the old woman, soaking her, frilly green hat first, black flat-soled clumpy shoes last.

Grijpstra, de Gier and Cardozo froze. They couldn't believe their eyes. What had been an aggressive body of sharp-tongued fury had changed into a sodden lump of wet flesh, and the lump stared at them. The old woman's face had been heavily made up and mascara was now running down each cheek, mixing with powder in reddish black-edged streaks which were getting closer and closer to her thin chiseled lips.

The silence was awkward.

Their neighbor, the vegetable man, had been staring at the woman too.

"Laugh, lady," the vegetable man said. "For God's sake, laugh, or we'll all cry."

The old woman looked up and glared at the vegetable man. "You . . ."

"Don't say it, lady," Grijpstra said, and jumped close to her, taking her by the shoulders and carrying her with him. "Go home and change. We are sorry about the water but it was the wind. You can blame the wind. Go along, lady, go home." The old woman wanted to free herself and stop, but Grijpstra went on pushing her, patting her shoulder and keeping up his monologue. "There now, dear, go home and have a nice bath. You'll feel fine afterward. Get yourself a big cup of hot tea and a biscuit. You'll be fine. Where do you live, dear?"

The old woman pointed at a side street.

"I'll walk you home."

She smiled. Grijpstra was very concerned. She leaned against the big solid man who was taking an interest in her, the first man she had been close to in years, ever since her son had died and she had been left alone in the city where nobody remembered her first name, living off her old age pension and her savings, and wondering when the social workers would catch her and stick her into a home.

"There you are," Grijpstra said at the door. "Don't forget your hot bath now, dear."

"Thank you," the old woman said. "You don't want to come up, do you? I have some good tea left, in a sealed tin. I have had it for years but it won't have lost its taste."

"Some other day, dear," Grijpstra said. "I have to help my mates. The sun has come back and we'll be busy this afternoon. Thanks anyway."

"You saved us all," de Gier said when Grijpstra returned. "The old cow would have murdered us. She had a wicked-looking umbrella."

"She never bought the lace," Cardozo said.

They were busy all afternoon, selling most of the cloth they had brought. Grijpstra and de Gier wandered about, leaving Cardozo to do the work, only coming back to the stall when the young detective's screams for help became too frantic. Grijpstra talked to Louis Zilver and de Gier followed up on their contact with the vegetable man. The hawkers were talking about Abe Rogge's death and the detectives listened but no new suggestions were given. There seemed to be a general feeling of surprise. The street sellers had all liked Rogge and were telling tall stories about him, stories which showed their admiration. The detectives were trying to find traces of envy in the conversation but there didn't seem to be any. The hawkers had enjoyed Rogge's success, success as a merchant, success with women. They mentioned his good breeding and his knowledge. They talked about the parties he had thrown in bars and at his home. They had lost a friend, a friend who had lent them money in times of stress, who had drawn customers to their corner of the market, who had listened to their troubles and who had cheered them up by his funny stories and extravagant way of behavior.

"We ought to do something tonight," the vegetable

man said. "Have a few drinks together in his honor. Least we can do."

"Shouldn't we wait for the funeral?" the vegetable man's wife asked.

"The body is still with the police," Louis Zilver said. "I phoned them this morning. They won't release it for a few more days."

"Let's have the party tonight," the vegetable man said. "I live close by. You can all come at about nine o'clock if my wife is willing. All right, wife?" The fat little woman agreed.

"We'll bring a bottle," Grijpstra said.

"Yes. It'll be in your honor too then," the vegetable man said. "You helped me out today and I hope you'll keep on coming here. I'll ask all the others around here. It'll be a big party, forty or fifty people maybe."

His wife sighed. He leaned over and kissed her cheek. "I'll help you clean up, darling, and we won't work tomorrow. We have cleared our stocks and we shouldn't work every day."

"Right," the vegetable man's wife said, prodding him affectionately.

16

THERE WEREN'T too many buyers around at four o'clock that afternoon and the street sellers began to clear their stalls, pleased with the day's results. The rain hadn't lasted long enough to spoil sales, the puddles had drained away and were dried by the hot sun, vegetables and flowers had sold well and the date was close enough to payday to create demand for durable goods. Even antiques and high-priced electrical appliances hadn't done badly. The hawkers were smiling as they loaded their minibuses, vans and trailers, and were feeling the weight of their wallets, tins and linen moneybags with some satisfaction.

"Right," Cardozo said, and lifted the remnants of a bale of cloth with a gesture of exuberance, but he over-did it and the end of the bale knocked a glass of coffee over, spilling the foaming liquid into the tin till which de Gier was about to close, having counted its contents.

"No," de Gier said.

"Silly," Grijpstra said as he bent down to survey the damage. "There's close to two thousand guilders in small notes in there. I have counted it too. Police money."

"No," de Gier said again. "We'll never get it dry and if it sticks together too much the bank won't accept it. You're a fool, Cardozo."

"Yes," Cardozo said. "You are right. You are always right. It's very annoying for other people, you know. You should learn to be wrong sometimes."

"You did it, you fix it," Grijpstra said. "Take it home and dry it somehow. You're still living with your parents, aren't you?"

"What's that got to do with it, adjutant?"

"Your mother may know of a way to dry it. Hang it on a line maybe, in the kitchen, with clothes pins. Or she can put it in the dryer. You've got a dryer at home?"

"The dryer may shred it," Cardozo said and dug about in the mess with his fingers. "It's all soddy now, it's only paper, you know."

"Your problem," de Gier said cheerfully. "You take care of it, constable. You can go home now and take the tin. We'll take care of the van. See you tonight at the party. Off you go."

"But . . ." Cardozo said, using the whining voice which he reserved for desperate occasions.

"Off," Grijpstra said. "Shoo! You heard what the sergeant said."

"He's only one rank above me. I am a constable first class."

"An adjutant is telling you too," de Gier said, "and an adjutant is two ranks above you. Off!"

"Yes, sir," Cardozo said.

"Don't cringe," de Gier said.

"No, sir."

"He always overdoes everything," Grijpstra said as they watched Cardozo's small shape, the till clutched in his arm, strutting away into the crowd.

De Gier agreed "He hasn't been in the police long enough. The police underdo things."

"As long as they are ruled by a democratic government."

De Gier turned around. "I thought you secretly preferred communism, Grijpstra."

"Ssh," Grijpstra said, looking around him stealthily. "I do, but the communism I like is very advanced. By the time society is ripe for it we won't need any police."

"You think the day will ever come?"

"No," Grijpstra said firmly, "but I can dream, can't I?"

"What will you do when the dream comes true?"

"I'll paint," Grijpstra said, and heaved the last bale of cloth into the gray van.

They were driving through Amsterdam's thick late-afternoon traffic when Grijpstra touched de Gier's forearm.

"Over there, on the right, near that lamppost."

A man was staggering about, trying to reach the wall. As de Gier watched he saw the man going down on his knees, crumpling up on the pavement. The man was well dressed, about fifty years old. They were close when the man's head hit the ground. They saw the top plate of his dentures fall out; they could almost hear the click when the plastic teeth touched the stone tile.

"Drunk?" de Gier asked.

"No," Grijpstra said. "He doesn't look drunk. Ill, I would say."

De Gier felt under the dashboard for the van's microphone and switched the radio on as Grijpstra put up its volume. The radio began to crackle.

"Headquarters," de Gier said.

"Headquarters," the radio voice said. "Come in, who are you, haven't you got a number?"

"No. We are in a special car, on special duty. Van Wou Street number 187. A man has collapsed in the street. Send an ambulance and a patrol car."

"Ambulance alerted. Is that you, de Gier?"

De Gier held the microphone away from his mouth.

"Stupid bugger," he said softly, "knows my name. I've got nothing to do with this."

"Yes, de Gier here."

"You take care of it, sergeant. We don't have a patrol car available right now. The traffic lights in your area aren't working properly and all available men are directing traffic."

"O.K.," de Gier said sadly, "we'll take care of this."

They could hear the ambulance's siren as they double-parked the van, obstructing traffic and drawing shouts from bicyclists who had to try to get around it.

"Park the van somewhere else," Grijpstra said, opening his door. "I'll see to this and you can join me later."

The man was trying to get back to his feet as Grijpstra knelt down, supporting his shoulders.

"What's wrong with you?"

"Nothing," the man said, slurring his words. "Felt a bit faint, that's all. I'll be all right. Who are you?"

"Police."

"Leave me alone, I don't need the police."

The man picked up his teeth and put them back into his mouth. He was trying to focus his eyes but Grijpstra's bulky shape wasn't more than a blurr.

"What do we have here?" the health officer was asking, bending down to sniff the man's breath. "Haven't been drinking, have we?"

"Don't drink," the man said. "Stopped years ago, only a glass of wine with my meals now. Felt a bit faint, that's all. Want to go home."

The health officer felt the man's pulse, counting and looking at Grijpstra at the same time.

"Police," Grijpstra said. "We happened to see this man staggering about and then he fell. What's wrong with him, you think?"

The health officer pointed at his heart and shook his head.

"Serious?"

The health officer nodded.

"You'd better go into the ambulance, sir." Grijpstra said.

"Never. I want to go home."

"Can't take him if he doesn't want to go, you know."

"Hell," Grijpstra said. "He is ill, isn't he?"

"Very ill."

"Well, take him then."

"If you say so," the health officer said, "and I'll want to see your identification."

Grijpstra produced his wallet, searched about in it and found his card.

"Adjutant H. Grijpstra, Municipal Police," the health officer read.

"What happens if we leave him here?"

"He may die and he may not. Most probably he will die."

"As bad as that?"

"Yes."

The man was on his feet now, looking perfectly all right.

"You are sure?"

"I am sure he is in very bad shape."

"Into the ambulance with you," Grijpstra snapped at the man. "I am ordering you to go into the ambulance. I am a police officer. Hurry up."

The man glared. "Are you arresting me?"

"I am ordering you to get into the ambulance."

"You'll hear about this," the man snarled. "I'll lodge a protest. I am going into the ambulance against my will. You hear?"

Together with the health officer Grijpstra pushed the man into the car.

"You'd better follow us in case we have complications," the health officer said. "You have a car with you?"

"Yes. What hospital are you taking him to?"

"Wilhelmina."

"We'll be there."

De Gier turned up and together they walked to the van. They arrived at the hospital a quarter of an hour later. The man was sitting on a wooden bench in the outpatients' department. He looked healthy and angry.

"There you are. You'll hear about this. There's nothing wrong with me. Now will you let me go home or not?"

"When the doctor has examined you," Grijpstra said, sitting down next to the man.

The man turned around to say something but seemed to change his mind, grabbing the back of his neck with both hands and going pale.

"Doctor," Grijpstra shouted. "Help! Nurse! Doctor!"

The man had fallen over his lap. A man in a white coat came rushing through a pair of swinging doors. "Here," Grijpstra shouted. The man was pulled to his legs with a nurse supporting him. The shirt was ripped off his chest and he was thumped, with all the force the man in the white coat could muster. He was thumped again and again and life seemed to return briefly before it ebbed away completely.

"Too late," the white-coated man said, looking at the body, which now slumped in Grijpstra's arms.

"Dead?" de Gier asked from the other corner of the room. The white-coated man nodded.

But another attempt was made to revive him. The body was roughly lifted and dumped on a bed. A cumbersome apparatus appeared, pushed in on wheels. The man's tattered shirt was torn off completely and the machine's long rubber-lined arms connected with the man's chest. The white-coated man turned dials and the body jumped, flinging its limbs away and up and down. The face seemed alive again for a brief moment but when the dial was turned again the body fell back, the eyelids no longer fluttered and the mouth sagged.

"No good," the white-coated man said, looking at Grijpstra. He pointed at a door. "In there, please. There are some forms to be filled in, about where you located him and how and so on. I'll see if we can find them. You are police officers, I assume."

"Yes!"

"I won't be a minute."

But he was several minutes, close to half an hour in fact. De Gier paced the room and Grijpstra studied a poster showing a sailboat with two men in it. The photo-

graph was taken from a helicopter or a plane for it
showed the boat from above, a white boat in a vast
expanse of water. De Gier came to look at the poster
too.

"Some people sail boats," de Gier said. "Other people wait in rooms."

"Yes," Grijpstra said slowly. "Two men in a boat. It
looks as if they are in the middle of the ocean. They
must be good friends, very close. Depending on each
other. The boat is too big for one man to handle. A
schooner, I think it is."

"Yes?" de Gier asked. "Are you interested in boats?"

"I am interested in solving our case," Grijpstra said.
"Do you remember that painting in Abe Rogge's room?
We saw it two days ago when we were taken by his
sister to see the corpse. There were two men in that
boat."

"So?"

The white-coated man came in with the forms and
they filled them in carefully, signing them with a flour-
ish.

"The man was a lawyer," the white-coated man said.
"We identified him from the papers he had in his wallet. A pretty famous lawyer, or infamous if you prefer
because he handled nasty cases only, charging a lot of
money."

"Died of natural causes, did he?" de Gier asked.

"Perfectly natural," the white-coated man said.
"Weak heart. Started to fibrillate. May have lived a
heavy life, overworked perhaps and too many rich
meals and expensive wines."

"And callgirls," de Gier said.

"Could be," the white-coated man said.

17

"BERT," the vegetable man said. "My name is Bert. They started calling me Uncle Bert some years ago but that isn't really my name. My name is Bert."

The detectives were shaking their host's scaly right hand in turns, mumbling their first names. "Henk," Grijpstra said. "Rinus," de Gier said. "Isaac," Cardozo said. They had arrived a little late and the house was full, filled with sweating street sellers and liquor fumes and the harsh acrid smoke of black shag tobacco rolled into handmade cigarettes. The house was close to the wide IJ River, right in the center of Amsterdam. A huge oil tanker was coming past, filling each window with its rusty bulk, honking its high-powered hooter moodily, like a lonely male whale complaining about its solitude.

"Beautiful house you've got here, Bert," Grijpstra said. "There won't be too many people in the city who've got such a clear view of the river as you have here."

"Not bad, hey? The house has been in the family

since my great-grandfather built it. Could get a good
price for it now, but why sell if you don't have to?
The vegetable business is bringing in the daily penny
and the wife and I've got a bit in the bank and no mortgage to worry about and the children all gone and
settled. What ho! Like a beer?"

"Yes," Grijpstra said.

"Or a shot from the big gun? I've got some jenever
that will make your ears wave and it's nice and cold
too. You won't be able to drink it all night but a snort
to set you off maybe?"

"I'll have a snort," Grijpstra said, *"and* a beer."

Bert slapped his thigh. "That's what I like. You're
like me. I always want everything. If they give me a
choice, that is."

"If I may," Grijpstra said, remembering the manners
which his mother had once tried to hammer into him.

"You may, you may," Bert said, and steered his guest
to a large trestle table loaded with bottles and plates
heaped with large green gherkins, shining white onions,
fat hot sausages and small dishes filled with at least ten
varieties of nuts.

"Nuts," Grijpstra shouted. "Nice."

"You like nuts?"

"Favorite food. I am always buying them but they
never reach my house. I eat them from the bag on the
way."

"Eat them all," Bert said. "I've got more in the kitch-
en. Heaps of them."

Grijpstra ate, and drank, and was grateful he had
been too late for his dinner and had refused Mrs. Grijpstra's grumpy offer to warm up the cheap dried beef
and glassy potatoes she had fed her family that night.
The jenever burned in his throat and the nuts filled his
round cheeks as he studied the room where de Gier,
immaculate in a freshly laundered denim suit and a pale
blue shirt, smoking a long thin cigar which accentuated
his aristocratic nose and full upswept mustache, was
listening to a middle-aged woman, flapping her artificial eyelashes. Cardozo was studying a TV set which

showed a dainty little girl being pursued by a tall thin blackhaired man through an endless and overgrown garden.

The room was as full of furniture as it was of people and it was only after his third glass of jenever that Grijpstra could accept its wallpaper, gold foil printed with roses the size of cauliflowers. There was no doubt about it, Uncle Bert was well off. It was also clear that he wasn't paying his taxes. Grijpstra turned and flattened his left hand and picked half a dozen nuts each from the ten small dishes with his right. The job took some time, and as the time passed Grijpstra thought and when Grijpstra had finished thinking he had decided that he didn't care about Uncle Bert's tax paying. His left hand was full now and he swept its contents into his mouth and chewed.

"You like music?"

Grijpstra nodded.

"I bought a record player the other day," Uncle Bert said, and pointed at a corner of the room. The corner was filled with a collection of electronic boxes, each one with its own set of knobs and dials, and connected to loudspeakers, which were pointed out one by one.

"I'll put on a record," Uncle Bert said. "The sound is magnificent. You can hear the conductor scratch his arse."

"Is that all he does?" Grijpstra asked.

"That's what he does before the music starts. Scratch, scratch and then 'tick' (that's his baton, his little stick you know) and then VRRAMMM, that's the tuba. It's nice music, Russian. Lots of brass and then voices. They sing fighting songs. I like the Russians. They'll come one day and do away with the capitalists here. I've been a member of the party all my life. I've been to Moscow too, six times."

"What's Moscow like?" Grijpstra asked.

"Beautiful, beautiful," Uncle Bert said, and spread his large hands. "The metro stations are like palaces, and all for the people, like you and me, and they play good football down there, and the market is better."

"But you can't make a profit."

Uncle Bert's eyes clouded as he refused to let the thought in. "Yes, yes."

"No," Grijpstra said. "They won't let you make a profit. They all get the same wage. No private initiative."

"It's a good street market, and the vegetables are better. Here. I'll play that record for you."

The record started. There was too much noise around for them to hear the conductor's scratching but when the tuba broke loose the room was drowned in sound and the guests were looking at each other, still moving their mouths, dazed by the unexpected clamor and wondering what was hitting them.

"KAROOMPF KAROOMPF," the tuba grumped, and the tall thin man was still chasing the dainty girl through the endless overgrown garden, in glaring color, on a screen the size of a small tablecloth. Grijpstra put his glass down and shook his head. His spine seemed suddenly disconnected, each vertebra rattled free by the combined attack of raw alcohol and brass explosions. A choir of heavy voices had come in now, chanting a bloodcurdling song in words which seemed to consist of vowels linked by soft *zylee*'s and *zylaa*'s. Uncle Bert was dancing by himself in the middle of the room, his eyes closed and his mouth stretched in a smile of pure ecstatic bliss.

"What . . ." Grijpstra began, but he let the question go. He would have a beer, he thought, and drink it slowly.

Cardozo thumped de Gier's back. He thumped too hard and the whisky which de Gier had been holding spilled down the dress of the middle-aged woman, who was still trying to talk to him. There had been ice cubes in the whisky and the woman shrieked merrily, trying to dislodge the ice cubes between her large breasts and mouthing some inviting words which nobody could hear.

De Gier spun around, drawing back his fist, but Cardozo smiled and pointed at the window, beckoning to de Gier to follow him. They passed the TV on their way. The tall thin man had caught the girl and had his hands around her slim lovely neck. The man and the girl were still in the overgrown endless garden, close to a stone outhouse, greenish white and lit up by the moon. The girl struggled and the man leered. The warrior's chant was swelling into a gigantic crescendo and tubas, trumpets, bassoons and clarinets honked and wailed shrilly in turn, framing the voices which were coming closer and closer as the girl's lace collar was being slowly torn away.

They had arrived at the window and de Gier saw two large parrots, one gray and one red, each in its own cage.

"Listen," Cardozo shouted.

De Gier went closer to the cages. Both parrots were jumping on their narrow wooden swings. The gray parrot seemed to be singing but the other was throwing up.

"He is puking," de Gier shouted.

"No. He is only making the sound. Uncle Bert told me. Uncle Bert was sick some days ago and the red parrot has been imitating him ever since. He does it very well, I think. Listen."

But de Gier had escaped. He didn't want to hear a parrot vomit. He was in the corridor, away from the noise, wiping his face with his handkerchief.

"I am getting drunk," de Gier thought. "I don't want to get drunk. Must drink water from now on. Lemonade. Cola. Anything."

There was a telephone in the corridor and he dialed his own number, steadying himself against the wall with his other hand.

"This is the house of Mr. de Gier," the telephone said.

"Esther?"

"Rinus."

"I am glad you came. I am at a mad party but I'll try to get home as quick as I can. How are you feeling?"

"Fine," Esther's low voice said. "I am waiting for you. Oliver has vomited all over the house. He must have been eating the geranium leaves, but I have cleared it all up now. He was asleep on my lap when you phoned."

"He always eats the geranium leaves. I am sorry he made a mess."

"I don't mind, Rinus. Will you be very long? Are you drunk?"

"I will be if I go on drinking but I won't. I'll be as quick as I can. I wouldn't be here if it wasn't work."

"Do you love me?"

"Yes. I love you. I love you more than I have ever loved anything or anybody. I love you more than I love Oliver. I'll marry you if you want me to."

He was still wiping his face with his handkerchief.

"You say that to all the girls."

"I've never said it before in my life."

"You say that to all the girls too."

"No, no. I have never said it. I've always explained that I don't want to marry, before I got too close. And I didn't want to marry. Now I do."

"You are crazy."

"Yes."

"Come home quickly."

"Yes, dear," de Gier said and hung up.

"Talking business?" Louis Zilver asked. He had just come into the corridor. Zilver was shaking his head, vainly trying to get rid of the noise in the room.

"Some party," de Gier said. "They are driving me mad in there. Are their parties always like that?"

"First time I have been to a party outside Abe Rogge's house for a long time. Abe's parties were always well organized, and he would have live music. A few jazz musicians who followed the mood of the evening, not like this canned stuff they are pouring out now. And the drinking was slower. They fill up your glass in here when the last drop is still on your lips. I haven't been going for more than an hour and I am sloshed already."

"They scare me in there," de Gier said. "I had to get away for a minute and speak to some sane person."

"I am sane," Zilver said. "Talk to me. You said they scare you. Do you really get scared sometimes?"

"Often."

"Anything in particular that scares you?"

"Blood," de Gier said, "and rats. Rats I can stand now. I saw one the other night when we were chasing someone near the river and I didn't mind so much. A big brown brute, he jumped into the water as I was almost on top of him. I wasn't really afraid then, but blood always gets me, I don't know why."

"You'll grow out of it," Zilver said and smiled at a girl who passed them to go to the toilet. "I am scared of things I can't define. I dream of them but I can't remember them when I wake up. I think I'll go back in there and chase a few girls."

"Switch the TV off," de Gier said. "They have some horror movie on. I would switch it off myself but I don't want to be rude. You know Uncle Bert better than I do."

"I will. I'll change the record too. We want some rock music if we are going to chase the girls. Some pretty ones came in just now. You want me to introduce you?".

"No, thanks. I am here to work."

"Good luck. Got any idea yet?"

"Lots of ideas," de Gier said, "but I want more than ideas."

Zilver smiled and closed the door behind him.

The girl had come out of the toilet and de Gier nipped in, locking the door with exaggerated care. He washed his hands carefully and combed his hair. He adjusted the silk scarf which was just the right color to go with his shirt. He sat down on the toilet seat and took out his pistol from its shoulder holster. He pulled out the clip and checked the cartridges. Six. He put the clip back and loaded, checking the breech. He could see the cartridge gleaming inside the steel of the barrel. He pulled the breech back and made the cartridge jump free. What am I doing this for? he thought. I never do this. He put the cartridge into the clip, replaced the clip and stuck the pistol back into its holster, washed his face, sat down again and lit a cigarette. Two corpses in two days. Three, counting the lawyer. But the lawyer had died because he had died. The others had been robbed of their lives. Robbery is a crime. Theft of the greatest good. The greatest good is life. And here he was, in a house filled with people thumping the floor with their great ungainly feet to the beat of doped long-haired young men, tearing at the atmosphere with their electric sound boxes and magnified drums. The killer might be in the room, thumping the floor too, drinking high-powered jenever and sucking a fat cigar, with his red hand on some woman's eagerly trembling bottom. Or would he be somewhere else in town, grinning to himself? Or herself? He hadn't seen the two women whom Grijpstra and the commissaris had interviewed. He had asked Grijpstra about them but he had only been given the gist of the conversation and a description of the women. He had a feeling that Grijpstra was following some other line of thinking and getting nowhere, for he was saying even less than usual. De Gier got back into his own line of thought. A ball, attached to a string. And the string attached to what? How could the ball have found its mark with such deadly precision?

And the commissaris? Did he know anything yet? The case was only a few days old. No need to rush. Work along the rules. Follow each possibility as far as it will go. Turn back if there is no result.

Someone knocked on the door.

"Coming," de Gier shouted and opened the door.

It was the middle-aged lady who had been talking to him before.

"Are you all right?" the woman asked, touching his shoulder. Her eyelashes shot up and came down slowly. "I was missing you in there."

"I am fine," de Gier said quickly. "Go ahead, dear. The toilet is all yours." He ran back into the room.

Zilver was talking to Grijpstra. Grijpstra's face was flushed and there was a full glass of beer in his hand.

"Rinus," roared Grijpstra, "how are you my boy? Jolly party this. Eat some of the nuts. Delicious nuts."

Zilver wandered off.

"I'll be going soon," de Gier said. "Will you be staying long?"

"Yes, I don't have anything else to do tonight and this isn't a bad way to spend the time."

"You are getting drunk."

"Yes." Grijpstra nodded gravely. "Drunk as a coot. Maybe I'd better go too. How is Cardozo?"

"Drinking lemonade and watching the parrots."

"Disgusting birds," Grijpstra said solemnly. "That red one is throwing up all the time."

"I know. What happened to the girl who was being throttled by the bad man?"

"Police came. Just in time. They always come just in time. To catch the bad man."

"Yes. We don't. Poor Elizabeth."

"Elizabeth?"

"The policeman who was an old lady."

"Oh, him. Transsexual fellow." Grijpstra had some trouble with the word. "Trans-sexual." He tried again.

"I met her," de Gier said, grabbing a glass of jenever from the table without being aware of it. "Nice person. Great friend of the commissaris. She had just finished a bellpull in half cross-stitch."

"Really?" Grijpstra's eyes were round and kind. "Half cross-stitch?"

"You are drunk," de Gier said. "Let's get out of here. I'll tip off Cardozo as we leave."

"Right," Grijpstra said, putting his glass down with such force that it broke. "Home. Or maybe I'll go to Nellie."

"Phone first. She may have a customer."

Grijpstra phoned twice. Nellie was free and a taxi was on its way. He came back looking so happy that de Gier ruffled his superior's short graying hair.

"Nice," Grijpstra said. "Very nishe. Nice, I mean."

Cardozo nodded when de Gier had finished whispering.

"What are you going to do?" Cardozo asked.

"Home. To bed."

"And the adjutant?"

"To bed."

"It's always me," Cardozo said. "Always. I spent an hour hanging all that money on the clothesline. My mother is furious with me for she's got to sit in the kitchen watching it dry. She thinks someone will come and steal it."

De Gier grinned.

"Not funny, sergeant. How long do you want me to stay here?"

"Till it's all over."

"Can I drink?"

"If you are careful. Don't blab. Just listen."

The red parrot had begun to throw up again. Cardozo closed his eyes.

"You'll be a sergeant one day, Cardozo, and then you can push another constable around."

"I will," Cardozo said. "Oh, I will!"

18

"TELL ME," the commissaris said.

The commissaris looked fresh, almost jolly, and sur-
prisingly elegant, for he had finally given in to his
wife's constant urging and put on his new linen suit to
go with the warm weather. It was specially cut for him
by a very old tailor who, in his young days, had
designed suits for the great merchants who made their
wealth in what was once called the Dutch East Indies.
The suit fitted him perfectly, somehow managing to look
loose and soft, and the thick golden watch chain span-
ning his waistcoat added to his general aura of luxury.
The commissaris had spent an evening, two nights and
a full day in bed, leaving it only to soak in a scaldingly
hot bath; and his wife had fussed over him continuously,
supplying him with coffee and orange juice and at least
five different soups, served in bowls with a plate of hot
toast on the side, and lighting his cigars for him (even
biting off the ends and spitting them out with a look of
gentle disgust); and the pain had finally left him so that
he could now sit in his oversized office and stretch

out his legs without having to worry about sudden
stabs and pricks and cramps, and take care of whatever came his way. De Gier had come his way that
morning, at nine sharp, the earliest anybody could
bother the commissaris in his secluded room. De Gier
was upset, pale in the face, and unusually nervous.

"What happened, de Gier?" the commissaris asked
again.

"A rat," de Gier said. "A large dead white rat. Its
belly was ripped open and its inside hung out and it
was covered in blood, and it was lying on my doormat
when I wanted to leave this morning. I would have
stepped on it if Oliver hadn't warned me. Oliver went
out of his mind when he saw the rat. His fur was all up.
He was twice his ordinary size. Like this."

De Gier indicated the size of Oliver. His hand was
about four feet off the floor.

"Really?" the commissaris asked. "That's very big
for a cat. Was he jumping up and down perhaps?"

"No. Neither was the rat. It just lay there. It had
been put there to annoy me. We don't have rats in the
building and if we did have rats they would be brown.
This was a white rat, the kind they use in laboratories.
I've got it with me, in a shoebox. Shall I show it to
you?"

"Later," the commissaris said.

The commissaris picked up his phone, dialed two
numbers and ordered coffee. He also offered de Gier
a cigarette and lit it for him. De Gier didn't thank the
commissaris; he was staring at the floor.

"Right," the commissaris said cheerfully. "So why
would anyone put a dead rat on your doormat, and kill
it first, and rip its entrails out? Do you have any disturbed friends who would play a prank on you? Only
your friends know that you are upset by the sight of
blood and corpses. Is there anyone in the police who
would do that to you? Think."

"Yes, sir."

"Perhaps you irritated some one."

"Cardozo," de Gier said. "I annoyed him yesterday.

Twice I annoyed him. I made him take the money from the market home because he had spilled coffee over it. It had to be dried, and last night at the party I made him stay after Grijpstra and I left."

The commissaris picked up the phone again. "Cardozo? Good morning, Cardozo, would you care to step into my room a minute?"

"No," Cardozo said, sitting on the edge of his chair. "Never. I wouldn't do that. I have never killed anything. I shot a man in the legs three years ago and I still have dreams about it. Bad dreams. I wouldn't kill an animal. And I like the sergeant."

De Gier looked up. "You do?" he asked in a tired voice. Cardozo didn't look at him.

"I am frightened of rats," de Gier said. "Blood upsets me, and rats too. A bloody rat is about the worst thing I can imagine. And there it was, right on my doormat. I only bought that doormat a few days ago. The old one was getting tatty. I can throw this one away too now."

"Yes," the commissaris called, answering a knock on the door.

"Morning, sir." Grijpstra closed the door carefully behind him and ambled into the room, waiting for the commissaris to ask him to sit down. The commissaris indicated a chair. Grijpstra didn't sit down, he fell into the chair. The chair creaked.

"Shit," Grijpstra said.

The commissaris looked up irritably.

"I beg your pardon," he asked sharply.

"Shit, sir," Grijpstra said, "all over my doorstep this morning. Dogshit. Somebody must have gone to a lot of trouble collecting dogshit, with a little spade I suppose, and a bucket. Very early this morning when nobody was about. It was heaped in front of my doorstep, I was in it up to my ankles before I knew what I was doing. They had even pushed it under the door but my corridor is very dark and I didn't notice it as I left the house. Whoever did that must hate my guts."

"De Gier had a bloody rat on his doorstep," the commissaris said. Grijpstra looked at de Gier who was smiling faintly.

"Shit?" de Gier asked.

"You think that's funny, don't you?" Grijpstra asked and half rose from his chair. "You're an idiot, de Gier. You are always laughing and rolling about with mirth when I step into it. Do you remember when the sea gulls shat all over me some months ago? You were laughing so much you nearly fell over. I have never laughed when you went into your tantrums because there was a drop of blood somewhere. Never!"

The commissaris got up and stood between them. "Now, now, gentlemen, let's not get more nervous than we are already. The day hasn't even started yet. Who do you think could have done this to you, Grijpstra? Who knows that a dog's droppings will upset you and, mind you, whoever it is has a reason to shake de Gier as well, for he had a similar occurrence this morning. It must be somebody who knows you both very well and who has a good reason to get even with you."

Grijpstra had turned around and was looking at Cardozo. Grijpstra's brows had sunk low and there was an angry glint in his otherwise quiet and harmless blue eyes.

"No," Cardozo said. "Not me, adjutant. I wouldn't be scraping the street to collect dogshit. This is not like me at all. I assure you." Cardozo was on his feet too, gesturing wildly.

"Right. It wasn't you, Cardozo," the commissaris said pleasantly. "Why don't you order some coffee for the adjutant and yourself. Use the phone. My coffee machine is out of order."

It took the commissaris twenty minutes of patient questioning before they connected blood, rat and dog droppings to Louis Zilver and the party the previous night. De Gier, who had been fairly drunk, had to force his memory before he recalled Zilver's questions in the corridor of Uncle Bert's house, and Grijpstra was only prepared to admit a similar conversation with Louis Zilver after de Gier had mentioned his incident.

"Yes," Grijpstra said reluctantly. "I was in my cups a bit. Shouldn't have been but I was. That jenever knocked me off straightaway. He must have gotten it from an illegal distillery somewhere, pure alcohol with a bit of a taste, nearly burned my guts out. And that young fellow seemed harmless. We were talking about the horror movie which was on the TV and about what scares people and I said that I can't bear shit. He laughed, the silly bastard laughed, and he said that it would be unlikely that they would ever show a shit-film on TV."

"And then you said that that's all they show on the telly," de Gier said. De Gier was looking much better.

"How do you know? You weren't there when Zilver was talking to me."

"It's the obvious thing to say."

"Oh, so I only say the obvious, hey? You have exclusive rights to intellectual conversation?"

"That'll be enough of that," the commissaris said, and selected a cigar from the small tin on his desk. He bent down so that Grijpstra had to search his pockets for his lighter.

"Thank you, Grijpstra. So our idea to have a sniff at the street market paid off. I am glad you got yourselves invited to that party. Zilver must have underestimated your drunkenness last night. Obviously he thought you would have forgotten what you said to him. This is a direct link. We may as well try to follow it up."

"Not much to charge the man with, sir," Grijpstra said, "if we can ever prove it was he. Dirtying the public thoroughfare is a minor offense. We can't even arrest him if we do prove the charge. He must have done it in the early hours, after he went home from the party."

"He wanted to shake you," the commissaris said. "He knows you and de Gier are charged with the Rogge case, and poor Elizabeth's death as well. The two cases

go together, of course. If he can shake the hounds the
fox will get away."

"He must be the fox himself," de Gier said.

"Possibly," the commissaris said, "but not necessarily.
Louis Zilver dislikes the police. He told me that his
grandparents were taken from their house by the Dutch
police, during the war. The police must have handed
them over to the Germans and the Germans put them
on transport to Germany and eventually killed them.
But he blames us, the Amsterdam Municipal Police, and
rightly so. If he can get at you and the adjutant, he re-
pays some of the debt he thinks he has to his grandparents."

"I was a boy at the time, sir."

"Yes, but your personal guilt has nothing to do with
it. Hatred is never rational, especially a deep hatred
such as Zilver must be suffering from. I was jailed and
tortured by the Germans during the war and I have
to force myself now to give directions to young German
students who have lost their way. I associate the way
they speak and behave with the young SS soldiers who
once knocked six of my teeth out. That was over thirty
years ago; the students weren't even born then."

"But we are trying to solve the murder of his friend,"
Grijpstra said. "If he bothers us it must be because he
has killed Abe himself."

The commissaris shook his head and raised a finger.
"He was in the house when Abe died, wasn't he? Esther
Rogge said so. And Zilver said Esther was in the house.
If Zilver killed Abe Rogge, Esther, the victim's sister,
must have been his associate. I think we all agree by
now that the killer was outside, most probably on the
roof of that wrecked houseboat opposite the Rogge
house."

"Zilver could have nipped out, sir," de Gier said,
"and nipped in again afterward. I would like your per-
mission to arrest him and hold him for questioning. We
have a serious reason to suspect him now. We can hold
him for six hours if you give the word."

"Yes," Grijpstra said. "I agree, sir."

"Just because of the dog droppings and the bloody rat?"

"I have another reason, sir," Grijpstra said slowly. They all looked at the adjutant, who had stood up and was staring out of the window, his hands deep in his pockets.

"You can tell us, Grijpstra," the commissaris said.

"The painting in Abe Rogge's room, sir. Perhaps you remember the painting. It shows two men in a boat, a small boat surrounded by foamy water. It must have been late at night, the sky is nearly as blue as the sea, a blackish blue. Maybe there was a moon—sky and sea almost merge and the boat is the central point in the painting."

"Yes, yes," the commissaris said. "Go on, and look at us when you are talking."

"Sorry, sir." Grijpstra turned around. "But the main point of that painting is not the boat or the sea or the light, but the feeling of friendship. Those two men are very close, as close as people can get. They are drawn as two lines, but the lines join."

"So?"

"I don't mean a homosexual relationship."

"No," the commissaris said. "I know what you mean, and you are right, I think. I saw that painting too."

"Bezuur told us that the two men were himself and Rogge. He got all blubbery about it. Do you remember sir?"

"Yes. Yes, he was obviously suffering. Quite genuinely I thought."

"Yes, sir. Rogge had dropped him or fought with him or broken the relationship in some other way. I believe Esther told de Gier that her brother just stopped seeing him. But Bezuur didn't crack up, for he had other interests, his father's business, which he inherited, and great wealth. But Zilver would have had nothing if Rogge had dropped him."

"Yes," the commissaris said. "True. A mentally disturbed young man who relied completely on his stronger partner. But did we have any suggestion that Rogge was going to, or had already, broken his relationship with Zilver?"

"No, sir," de Gier suddenly said. "Or at least, not that I know of. But if he *had* it would certainly have upset Louis Zilver, and Zilver is capable of extraordinary activity when he gets upset. He proved that this morning, didn't he?"

"So," the commissaris said slowly. "You two are suggesting that Rogge told Zilver to go away, leave the house, get out of the partnership on the street market, and so forth. Esther said that Rogge would drop people the minute they began to bore him. He didn't need anybody apparently, and he could always find new company. A throng of admiring women, for instance. Flicked his fingers and they wagged their tails, so Tilda told us. The other lady confirmed the fact too. That Kops woman, the surrealist, huh!" He shuddered. "Silly woman that. But never mind. So he told Zilver to get lost and Zilver reacted drastically!"

"Indeed," Grijpstra said. "Esther also told us that Rogge liked to upset people, show them up for what they really are, prick their vanity. He must have done that to Zilver too. Maybe he did it once too often. And suddenly, without anyone being around to notice it. A single remark perhaps. Esther apparently doesn't suspect Zilver, because she didn't know that Abe had told him off. Zilver must have killed Rogge almost immediately after the incident happened."

"Now, now," the commissaris said. "And what about the device? He must have used a hellish machine, as de Gier pointed out before. An ingenious unusual weapon. Did he have it in his cupboard? And did he run to his room after Abe told him off? Did he grab the weapon, rush outside, use it and run back to his room again?"

"Sir," de Gier said.

"Yes, de Gier?"

"It must have been an ordinary thing, sir. A hellish machine which looks like an ordinary utensil."

The commissaris thought. He also grunted. "Yes. Because he had it outside in the street and the riot

police didn't notice anything amiss," the commissaris
said slowly.

"Zilver isn't normal, sir," Grijpstra said. "He is probably insane. This dogshit and bloody rat business proves
it. No sane person would go to such lengths as he must
have done early this morning. Poor fellow can't be
blamed, I suppose. The war, and what happened to his
grandparents and all that. If he is our man we'll have
to turn him over to the city psychiatrists. But I think
this is the moment to grab him. He'll probably know we
are after him and he'll be defensive and frightened and
ready to talk."

"True," the commissaris said.

"So can we have a warrant for his arrest, sir?"

"No," the commissaris said. "I am not convinced
that he committed a murder, or two murders. Whoever
killed Rogge killed Elizabeth. And whoever killed Elizabeth is ready to kill again. Maybe you are right, but I
doubt it."

"So do we forget the incident, sir?" There was no
emotion in Grijpstra's voice. He was rubbing the stubbles on his chin.

"Certainly not. You and I are going to see him."

"Excuse me, sir," Cardozo said.

"Yes?"

"Just a suggestion, sir. Why don't you let me go and
find him. I won't spill anything, just that I was told to
take him to Headquarters. Maybe he'll say something
to me on the way. He has nothing against me so far and
we are about the same age. We even have the same
background."

"Very well," the commissaris said. "Bring him in by
public transport. But make sure someone is following
you. And watch him. We don't know under what stress
he is laboring. And perhaps you and I should question
him. Grijpstra may provoke him into another tirade
about the police. On your way, Cardozo. Bring him
straight up to my room when you come back."

"Sir," Cardozo said, and left.

"That's better," Grijpstra said. "You are right, sir. I

am ready to wring his neck. And so are you," he added, looking at de Gier.

"Yes," de Gier said. "I've got that dead rat in a carton on my desk. I'll show it to you."

"Never," Grijpstra said. "Put that box in an ashcan. I am not showing you that dogshit, am I?"

"Gentlemen, gentlemen," the commissaris said. "I am sure there's something useful to do. Find out what it is and then do it. I'll let you know as soon as I know something."

19

"AM I UNDER ARREST?" Louis Zilver asked. He was sitting in a low leather chair, close to the window of the commissaris' office, and was frantically sucking smoke from a cigarette he had taken out of his own packet, after having refused the small cigar which the commissaris had offered him. Cardozo was in the chair next to him and the commissaris faced the two young men. The commissaris was sitting on his desk. He had had to jump to reach its top and his feet were off the ground.

"No," the commissaris said.

"So I can go if I want to?"

"Surely."

Louis jumped up and walked to the door. Cardozo followed him with his eyes, the commissaris looked at his cigar.

Louis waited at the door.

"Why don't you go?" the commissaris asked after a while.

Louis didn't answer.

"If you are going to stay you may as well sit down again."

"Yes," Louis said and returned to his chair.

"Well, now. You have upset two of my men this morning and I would like to know why you went to such trouble as you must have gone to. The rat, for instance."

"The rat?" Louis asked in a high voice.

"The rat," the commissaris repeated. "There are a lot of dog droppings in our streets, too many of them in spite of all our efforts to educate dog-owners to train their animals to use the gutters. I can see how you got the dog droppings, but the rat puzzles me."

"I didn't kill the rat. I found him in the courtyard. Esther's cat brought him in. I think he belonged to the little boy next door. I found him when I came back from the party and I remembered the sergeant's remark about rats. I took Abe's car and went to the sergeant's apartment. The address is in the phone book. I knew I had the right address, for Esther's bicycle was there."

"Esther Rogge?"

"Yes, the two of them have something going. I think the sergeant is making use of Esther, pumping her for information most probably, while he is putting on the charm. He's a very handsome man, your sergeant."

Cardozo grinned and the commissaris looked at him. Cardozo stopped grinning.

"Yes," the commissaris said, "de Gier has a way with women. But it never seems to get him anywhere. His only real contact is his cat, I think. But why bother the adjutant too? I can understand that you may think that you dislike the sergeant but the adjutant has given you no reason to . . ."

Zilver laughed. "It happened during the party. Both of them told me about their fears. I thought that I should finish the job properly."

"You certainly succeeded."

Zilver rubbed out his cigarette. "Are you going to do something about this? If you do I'll gladly pay the fine."

"No," the commissaris said and adjusted his watch

chain. "No, I think not. We are investigating two killings. I still think you may help us."

"You are the police," Zilver said, and looked at the Persian rug which dominated the center of the large room. "I see no reason why I should help the police."

"I see your point. Well, you are free to leave, as I have said before."

"Where were you during the war?" Zilver asked suddenly, sitting down again after he had half risen from his chair.

"I was in jail for three years."

"Where?"

"In Scheveningen jail."

"That's where they put the people from the Resistance, isn't it?"

"That's right, but I wasn't really in the Resistance. I was accused of disorganizing one of their transports to Germany and helping to hide deportees."

"Jews?"

"That's correct."

"And had you disorganized the transport?"

"Yes. They couldn't prove it but nobody asked for proof in those days."

"And you were in a cell for three years?"

"Yes."

"By yourself."

"For about seven months."

"Seven months, that's a long time."

"Fairly, and it wasn't a comfortable cell. There was some water in it. Caused my rheumatism, I think. But that's all over and done with now."

"No," Zilver said. "It isn't and it never will be. You still have your rheuma, don't you? I noticed you were rubbing your legs when you interrogated me before. You must still be in pain."

"Not today, and when I die the pain will go forever."

"Possibly," Zilver said.

"I didn't bring you here to discuss the commissaris' rheuma," Cardozo said irritably. "Your friend has been killed and a harmless old lady has been killed, and both by the same killer."

"Yes?" Zilver asked.

"Yes," the commissaris said. "We don't have many killings in the city and these two are linked. You knew Abe well. You knew the people Abe knew. You know the killer."

"You are only assuming things, you know."

"We don't know for sure," the commissaris admitted. "Would you like some coffee? Human thought is incapable of coming to absolute conclusions. You studied law and you know that. But sometimes we can assume with a certain degree of certitude. Like in this case."

"I'd like some coffee."

The commissaris looked at Cardozo who jumped to his feet and grabbed the telephone.

"Three coffees, please," Cardozo said, "in the commissaris' room."

"All right," Zilver said. "I know the killer. You know him too. And I know how Abe was killed but I only found out yesterday, by chance."

"You did?"

"He was killed by means of a fishing rod, a rod with a reel. A weight was attached to the end of the line."

Cardozo clapped his hands and Zilver looked at him.

"You couldn't figure it out, could you?"

"No," the commissaris said. "We got as far as a rubber ball, spiked with nails most probably, and attached to a string. Sergeant de Gier thought of it. He remembered having seen some little boys playing on the beach. They were hitting a ball with wooden bats and the ball was attached to a weight by an elastic band so that it couldn't get away, even if the boys missed it. How did you come to think of a fishing rod?"

The coffee was brought in and Zilver stirred his cup industriously.

"It's a new sport. I have a friend who fishes and he was telling me that he joined a club where they play with fishing rods. They attach a dart to the end of their line and then throw it, at a bull's-eye set up at some considerable distance. It's an official sport apparently and they even have tournaments. He said he was getting very good at it."

"Never heard of it," the commissaris said.

"I hadn't either. But it solved the crime for me. The killer must have stood on the houseboat opposite our house. He pretended to be fishing and the riot police who were patrolling the street took no notice of him. There are always people fishing in the Straight Tree Ditch and there were people fishing there right through the riots. When he saw his chance clear he turned around, flicked the rod and hit Abe. Abe may not have seen him, and if he did he may not have recognized him. The killer may have worn one of those shapeless plastic coats and a hat to go with it. Dressed like that and seen from the back, he would be unrecognizable, just another fisherman."

"So Abe knew the killer, did he?"

"Of course."

"Who was he?"

"Klaas Bezuur."

"You are sure, are you?"

"The human mind is incapable of coming to absolute conclusions," Zilver said, "but sometimes we can assume with a certain degree of certitude. Like in this case."

The commissaris smiled. "Yes. But you must have some information we don't have. We were told, by Esther, by you, and by Bezuur himself that Abe and Bezuur were close friends."

"They *were*," Zilver corrected.

"What happened?"

"Nothing specific. Abe dropped Bezuur because Bezuur dropped his freedom. He left Abe to become a millionaire in the earth-moving machine business. He got his big house and his Mercedes motorcar and his wife and his girl friends and his expensive holidays in three-star hotels and lived the high life. He stopped thinking and questioning."

"Did they fight? Or argue?"

"Abe never fought. He just dropped him. He was still borrowing money from Bezuur to finance his bigger transactions and paying it back and borrowing again, but that was purely business. Bezuur charged a stiff rate of interest. But there was no further real contact between them. Bezuur kept on trying, but Abe would laugh at him and tell him that he couldn't have it all. Rogge didn't mind Bezuur's wealth and expensive ways, but he minded Bezuur's weakness. They dropped out of the university together because they had decided that they were only being trained to accept an establishment which was incredibly foolish and wrong. They were going to find a new way of life, an adventure, a joint adventure. They would do crazy things together, like sailing a leaking boat through a full gale, and riding camels through North African deserts, and reading and discussing strange books, and traveling about in the Eastern European countries in an old truck. Abe told me once that they lost their first truck on their first trip. They had been tipped off that a Czechoslovakian factory was selling beads cheaply and they went out there, in winter. They bought all the beads the truck could hold, but the packing wasn't very good. The factory gave them some flimsy cartons, tied together with paper string. On the way back the roads were icy and the truck went into a spin and turned over. Abe said the beads stretched to the horizon and caught the light of the setting sun. He and Bezuur had jumped up and down and laughed and cried, the sight was so beautiful."

"And?" the commissaris asked.

"Well, they lost the merchandise and they lost the truck and they had to hitchhike back. Bezuur said that the moment had been very important to him. It had been some sort of awakening to the nonsense of human endeavor and the beauty of the creation. But he said that words couldn't describe the sensation."

"Hmm," the commissaris said doubtfully. "I met Bezuur, you know, and he didn't seem to have that quality. I can't imagine him jumping up and down in a white landscape covered with reflecting beads."

"No," Zilver said. "Exactly. He lost it. Abe said that Bezuur had been awake a little but he had managed to fall asleep again. He called him a hopeless case."

"And he dropped him?"

"Yes. Bezuur was still coming to the house but Abe would chase him away. He wouldn't even let him in, but would talk to him at the door. Abe could be very nasty if he wanted to. And there may have been other reasons. Bezuur loved Esther once and tried to get her. I think they did sleep together a few times but Esther didn't really want him, especially when he started trying to impress her with his motorcar and bungalow and the rest of it. He married a friend of hers but she couldn't stand him either. She is in France somewhere now, living in a hippie commune, I believe."

"So why didn't he kill Esther?"

"He could hurt her more by killing her brother. Abe was the sun in Esther's life."

"She's got another sun in her life now," Cardozo said.

"The sergeant?"

"Looks like it," the commissaris said.

"A policeman?" Zilver asked.

The commissaris and Cardozo studied Zilver's face and Zilver squirmed.

"Never mind," the commissaris said. "When did you find out that it must have been Bezuur?"

"Last night at the party. The friend who told me about the fishing-rod sport is a street seller. He came to the party and told me that Bezuur is in their club and that he is the champion. Bezuur is a good shot too. Abe kept an old rifle in his boat and he shot at floating bottles, out on the lake. I like doing that too. Abe always said that Bezuur was the best shot he ever met."

"Having a firearm nowadays is a crime," Cardozo said.

"Is that so?" Zilver asked. "Well, I never."

"Would you have told us about Bezuur?" the commissaris asked.

"No. But now I have anyway. I told you I would never help the police, and certainly not deliberately."

"Bezuur has now killed twice," the commissaris said, "and his other victim was an old lady who must have seen him hanging about the Straight Tree Ditch, some hours after he had killed Abe. He probably came back to see what the police were doing. He had even gone to the trouble of providing himself with an alibi. He had two callgirls at his house, poured full of champagne and fast asleep, but willing to swear that he had been with them. Perhaps he went back to kill Esther, or yourself. You took his place. To let a man like him wander about is to ask for trouble, serious trouble. A very dangerous man, highly intelligent and skilled in unusual ways and tottering on the verge of his sanity."

"The Germans are still wandering about," Cardozo said pleasantly. "Millions and millions of them. They are highly skilled and highly intelligent. They've started two major wars and they have killed so many innocent people that I couldn't visualize the figure, or even pronounce it. It's not only the Germans. The Dutch killed a lot of innocent Indonesians. Killing seems to be part of the human mind. Maybe Abe was right when he said that we don't control ourselves but are moved by outside forces, by cosmic rays perhaps. Maybe the planets are to blame, and should be arrested and destroyed."

The commissaris moved his feet, which were about a foot above the floor. Cardozo smiled. The commissaris reminded him of a small boy, at ease on a garden wall, engaged in playing his own game, which happened to be moving his feet at that particular moment.

"Interesting," the commissaris said, "and not as far-fetched as it seems, maybe. But still, we are here and we have our disciplines, and even if they lead nowhere in the end we can still pretend that we are doing something worth doing, especially if we are doing the best we can."

It was quiet in the room. The commissaris moved his feet together.

"Yes," he said. "We'll have to go and arrest Mr. Bezuur. Where would he be right now, do you think, Mr. Zilver?"

"Any of a dozen places," Zilver said. "I can give you a list. He may be at his office, or at home, or in any of the four yards where he keeps his machinery, or he may be wandering about in the Straight Tree Ditch area again."

"Would you like to come with us?" Cardozo asked, looking at the commissaris for approval. The commissaris nodded.

"Yes. I shouldn't have told you but I have, and now I wouldn't mind seeing the end of it."

The commissaris was telephoning. He spoke to Grijpstra, and to the police garage.

"We'll go in two cars," he said. "You and Cardozo can come with me in the Citroën. Grijpstra and de Gier will follow in their VW. Are you armed, Cardozo?"

Cardozo opened his jacket. The butt of his FN pistol gleamed.

"Don't touch it unless you absolutely have to," the commissaris said. "I hope he hasn't got his fishing rod with him. Its accuracy and reach will be about as much as those of our pistols."

"Mr. Zilver?"

Louis looked up.

"You can come with us on one condition. Stay in the background."

"All right," Zilver said.

20

THE TWO CARS left Police Headquarters at about eleven that morning and managed to lose contact almost immediately, as the constable at the wheel of the Citroën beat a traffic light just as it changed, leaving de Gier cursing in the battered VW, stuck behind a three-wheeled bicycle ridden by an invalid.

Grijpstra grunted.

"*You* should drive this car for a change," de Gier said, turning up the radio's volume.

"Yes?" the radio voice asked as de Gier gave his number.

"Put me on relay," de Gier said, "and give us another frequency. Your third channel is free, is it?"

"Fourth channel is free," the voice said. "I'll tell the commissaris' car to change into it."

"Yes?" the constable in the Citroën asked.

"Don't drive so spectacularly, constable," de Gier said. "We are still in Marnix Street and we have lost you already. Which way are you going?"

"East, through Weteringschans. We are headed for

a yard in the industrial part on the other side of the
Amstel."

"Wait for us, I'll try to catch up, and don't rush off
when you see us."

They found the Citroën again and tagged on. Bezuur
wasn't in the yard. He wasn't in the next yard either.
They tried his office. They went to the south but he
wasn't at home. De Gier's initial impatience disappeared. Grijpstra sat next to him, smoked his small
black cigars and said nothing, not even when a Mercedes, coming from the left, ignored their right of way
and made them lunge forward as de Gier kicked his
brake.

The radio came to life again. Cardozo's voice, flattened strangely, mentioned that it was past lunchtime.

"So?" de Gier asked.

"So the commissaris wants lunch."

Grijpstra broke his silence and grabbed the microphone from de Gier's hand.

"Excellent thought, Cardozo. Tell your driver to turn
right at the next traffic light, second right after that."

"What's there, adjutant?"

"A Turkish snack bar. They serve hot rolls with
some sort of a meat stew inside, and tomatoes and
onions."

The radio crackled for a while and the commissaris'
voice came through.

"These Turkish rolls you mentioned, Grijpstra, what
are they like?"

"Delicious, sir, but a little foreign."

"Spicy?"

"Not too much, sir."

"What's the restaurant's name?"

"A Turkish name, sir. Couldn't pronounce it if I
could remember it, but you can't miss it. They have
a stuffed donkey on the sidewalk and there's a Turkish
lady on the donkey, with a veil and wide trousers and
lots of necklaces."

"Yes?" the commissaris asked. "She's got to sit on
that carcass all day?"

"A dummy, sir, a window display model. Not alive."

"I see," the commissaris said.

They sat on the restaurant terrace and ate. The commissaris complimented Grijpstra on his good taste and ordered another helping. Zilver began to talk to de Gier and de Gier, after breathing deeply, managed to look friendly. Cardozo looked at the lady on the donkey. She seemed to be slipping off and he wanted to get up and adjust her, but then the commissaris asked for the bill.

"So where shall we go now, Mr. Zilver?"

"There's another yard in Amstelveen where he keeps some of his larger earthmovers and a few bulldozers and tractors. I've been there but I got the impression that he doesn't often go there himself, so I was keeping it as a last possibility."

"What were you doing there?" the commissaris asked. "You weren't particularly friendly with Klaas Bezuur, were you?"

"I wasn't," Louis said, "but I had nothing against the man either. He was lending us a lot of money after all. I went to the yard that time with Abe. Bezuur had phoned to tell us about a new bulldozer he had bought and which he wanted to demonstrate. I thought Abe wouldn't be interested, but he went straight off and I went with him. Corin Kops, one of Abe's girlfriends, went too. We played around all afternoon. He let us drive some of the machines. We even chased each other."

"Must be nice," de Gier said, "like playing with toy cars at the fair."

"Those machines aren't exactly toy cars," Zilver said. "Some of them must weigh a few tons. I was driving a mechanical digger that afternoon which had a mouth the size of a killer whale's."

"The yard is in Amstelveen, you say," the commissaris said. "Amstelveen isn't a suburb of Amsterdam. It's another city and outside our territory. Well, we can always plead that we were in hot pursuit."

Grijpstra looked doubtful.

"Yes, perhaps we shouldn't. If Mr. Zilver gives us the address we can alert the Amstelveen police. They can send a car out too. We'll make them feel they are in it as well."

Bezuur saw them coming, which was unfortunate. The yard was big, fifty by a hundred meters, and surrounded by a high brick wall, partly overgrown by a profusion of plants. Bezuur was standing right in the middle of the yard as Grijpstra and de Gier came in through the large swinging gates.

"Good day," de Gier shouted, and Bezuur was about to return the greeting when he caught a glimpse of Louis Zilver, getting out the black Citroën's rear door. He also saw the nose of the white police van which the Amstelveen constables were parking on the other side of the street.

Bezuur stopped, turned and ran.

"Halt," Grijpstra boomed, but Bezuur was already climbing onto a bulldozer. As the bulldozer's diesel engine started up, Grijpstra drew his pistol.

"Halt! Police! We'll shoot!"

The commissaris was with them now. The constable had come with him but turned and ran toward the Citroën as he saw the bulldozer coming closer. The constable opened the trunk of the Citroën and grabbed a carbine. He loaded and knelt near the swinging doors. Grijpstra had pointed his gun at the sky and fired. The constable fired too, but the bulldozer's great blade had come up and the bullet hit the blade and ricocheted wildly, burying itself in the brick wall and disturbing the leaves of a creeper, which shook its red flowers in feeble protest. De Gier was firing too but his bullets missed as the bulldozer spun around on its left track. The Amstelveen uniformed constables were hesitating near the gate, seeing little point in using their firearms with so much movement in front of them. The bulldozer roared and kept on turning, its gleaming heavy steel blade moving up and down. The blade stopped in a horizontal position, bare and menacing, and the machine sprang forward. De Gier broke out in a sweat. The bulldozer's blade was aimed at the commissaris, a small lost figure in the vast yard. He inserted his spare clip into the pistol and fired again. He saw Bezuur's fat bulk shake as the bullet hit him but the machine didn't falter, plodding on steadily toward the commissaris, who was running to the yard's nearest corner where, panting, he meant to find refuge by flattening himself against the wall bricks.

De Gier felt a hand on his shoulder and looked around. Cardozo was squatting next to him, pointing at the other side of the yard. Another engine had come to life, a great mechanical digger was coming forward, grinding the gravel with its huge tracks.

"Zilver," Cardozo shouted.

"What?"

"Zilver! He's in the cabin of the digger. I asked him to do something. He said he could handle the digger, didn't he?"

De Gier nodded, but he wasn't interested. He looked again at the commissaris, who had now reached the corner and seemed to be tearing at the creepers in a vain attempt to put more distance between his small body and the approaching blade. The corner seemed safe, for the blade scraped the walls at each side without being able to touch him. Creepers and trailers were being torn off the walls and fell on the blade and on Bezuur's seat, decorating the bulldozer with its red and orange flowers and dark green leaves. The bulldozer reversed and jumped forward again, grazing the wall this time, forcing the commissaris to give up his refuge. As the bulldozer turned to pursue the running old man, de Gier almost closed his eyes to blot out the scene. The commissaris didn't have a chance on open ground, he would never be able to outrun the bulldozer. De Gier emptied his clip but the bullets hit the machine, not the man directing its onslaught. When de Gier's pistol clicked he snarled at Cardozo. "Fire, you fool, fire."

Cardozo shook his head. "Grijpstra is behind there somewhere, look!"

The digger had found the bulldozer and its closed steel-toothed mouth was aimed at Bezuur's body. The digger's engine growled and they could see Zilver in his glass-covered cabin at the rear of the machine, frantically pushing levers. Bezuur felt the danger and made the bulldozer change direction. De Gier jumped up and raced toward the commissaris, who collapsed against him. De Gier picked the old man up and ran to the gate. A constable opened the rear door of the Citroën and de Gier lowered the commissaris onto the back seat.

"I am all right," the commissaris said. "Go back, sergeant. Bezuur is wounded already, we don't want to kill him. See if you can't get the digger to overthrow Bezuur's machine."

"Sir," de Gier said and ran back. When he got to the yard he saw the digger's teeth hit the back of Bezuur's head. Zilver had pushed his lever suddenly and moved it right over. The pointed spearlike teeth hit Bezuur with the full power of the diesel engine roaring away under Zilver's cabin. The head snapped free and was shot across the yard, hitting the stone wall and exploding against it. De Gier's legs weakened and he found himself lying in the yard with Cardozo tugging at his shoulders, for the bulldozer kept going along slowly and they were in its way.

"Up, up," Cardozo shouted and de Gier dumbly obeyed, dragging himself away. Grijpstra ran after the bulldozer, swung himself onto its saddle and turned the key on the small dashboard. Zilver had switched off the digger's engine. It was very quiet in the yard. De Gier heard the sparrows twittering among the creepers.

"Sparrows," de Gier said. "They have lost their nests in there."

"Sparrows?" Grijpstra asked. "What sparrows?"

De Gier pointed at the wall. The creepers were all down on one side, meshed into the ground by the bulldozer's tracks.

"Who cares about sparrows? That fool has lost his head."

Grijpstra pointed at Bezuur's fat body, lying on its back where it had fallen after the digger's mouth had hit it. Blood was still oozing out of its rump and they could see the heavy neck muscles, torn into a ragged circular edge.

De Gier's legs faltered again and Grijpstra's arm caught his shoulders.

A uniformed constable came running up.

"Are you in charge of this arrest?" the constable asked.

"The commissaris is in the car, constable," Grijpstra said, "in the Citroën. He is in charge, but I think you will have to write the report; this is your territory. You witnessed the proceedings, didn't you?"

"Proceedings," the constable muttered. "Proceedings! I've never seen anything like it in my life. What are we going to do about the fellow's head?"

"Scrape it off the yard and the wall and put it in a box," Grijpstra said. "And the man who handled the digger isn't ours but a civilian. We've got his name and particulars. Don't charge him, we have reason to be grateful; he saved the commissaris' life. I also have the name of the dead man for you."

Grijpstra took out his notebook, opened it and scribbled. He tore out the page and gave it to the constable. "If you want me you can reach me at Amsterdam Headquarters. Grijpstra is the name. Adjutant Grijpstra."

"I'll be wanting you," the constable said. "You'll have me on your back for the rest of the week. What a show! If we staged an arrest like this in Amsterdam, we would never hear the end of it."

"We're from the big city, constable," Grijpstra said. "Be grateful you live in the province."

Another constable had arrived.

"You," the first constable said, "get a knife or a small spade or something and a box. I want you to collect whatever you can find of the head."

"Bah," the other constable said.

Cardozo grinned. The first constable had three stripes, the second only two. Grijpstra grinned too.

"Poor fellow," Cardozo said.

The sparrows were still twittering as they left the courtyard.

21

"MY DEAR," she said, as the commissaris limped into his house. "Has it got worse again? I thought it had gone when you left this morning; you looked positively spry when you got into the car."

The commissaris mumbled something in which only the word "tea" stood out. "I am fine," he answered, "bumped into something, that's all."

"I'll make the tea in a minute. Oh, your *suit!*"

The suit was stained, it was also torn. A creeper had stuck to one of the sleeves as he had tried to pull himself free when the bulldozer came at him. He tried to cover the tear with his hand as she pulled him into the light near the window.

"And what's that? Blood?"

He remembered that he had stood close to the corpse.

"Yes," he said, "blood, dear, but it'll come off again and I am sure the old tailor can repair the suit. I would like some tea, and a bath. Will you bring up a tray?"

"Yes. Will you be long? You do remember that my

sister and her husband are coming tonight? They phoned this morning and I said you were much better."

The commissaris was halfway up the stairs. He stopped, turned and sat down.

"You won't mind, will you? They are always so nice and he wants to tell us about the firm he took over, a factory somewhere in the South. He's very excited about it."

"I do mind," the commissaris said. "Phone them and tell them I am ill. I want to smoke cigars tonight and sit in the garden and I want you to sit with me. We can listen to the turtle. He's very nice too, and he never takes over anything."

"My dear, you know I hate to tell lies."

The commissaris had got up again and was climbing the rest of the stairs. His wife sighed and picked up the telephone in the hall. She could hear the hot water being turned on in the bathroom.

"I am so sorry, Annie," she said, "But Jan's legs are much worse again. He's feeling terrible and I thought it might be better if we . . ."

Mrs. Grijpstra glared as the adjutant bit off the end of a small black cigar and spat it in the direction of the large copper ashtray standing on a side table in the corridor. He missed it by about a foot.

"The smoke is bad enough," she said, her voice rising dangerously. "You don't have to mess up the house as well. I've told you a thousand times . . ."

"Enough," Grijpstra said quietly.

"You are late again," she said. "Won't you ever be on time? I fried up the potatoes we had left over from yesterday. There are some in the pan. Do you want them?"

"Yes," Grijpstra said, "and some bread. And make a pot of coffee." His voice was low and she switched on the light in the corridor to be able to see his face.

"You are very pale. You aren't sick, are you?"

"I am not sick."

"You look sick."

"I am sick of my job," Grijpstra said, and stood. His arms dangled and his cheeks sagged. His wife's bloated face moved into what, twenty years ago, would have been a smile of compassion.

"Go and shave, Henk," she said. "You always feel better when you have shaved. I got a new stick of soap yesterday and there's a packet of blades I found behind the night table. They are extra sharp or something, it's that brand you couldn't get the other day when we went to the supermarket."

"Ah," Grijpstra said. "Good. I'll be ten minutes." He watched her waddling to the kitchen.

"Horrible blob of fat," he said as he opened the bathroom door. He was smiling.

"Ah, there you are," Mrs. Cardozo said, as her son came into the kitchen. "Did you deliver that money to the station?"

"Yes, mother."

"Did they count it?"

"Yes, mother."

"Was it all there?"

"Yes, mother."

"We're having fish for supper and sour beet roots."

"Yagh!" Cardozo said.

"Your father likes it and what's good enough for your father should be good enough for you."

"I hate sour beet roots, don't you have something else? A nice salad?"

"No. Did you have a good day?"

"We tried to arrest a man who was driving a bulldozer but his head got chopped off by a mechanical digger."

"Don't tell stories. You know I don't like you to tell stories."

"It's true. It'll be all over the front page of the *Telegraph* tomorrow."

"I don't read the *Telegraph*," his mother said. "Go and wash your hands. Your father will be home any minute now."

Cardozo washed his hands in the kitchen sink. His mother watched his back.

"Man driving a bulldozer indeed," she said.

Cardozo's back stiffened but he didn't turn around.

"You are late," Esther said. "I have to go home to feed *my* cat. I am sure Louis will forget."

De Gier embraced her, squeezing Oliver, who was upside down in Esther's arms and purring sleepily.

"You'll come again later, will you?"

"Yes, but it'll take me at least two hours. It's a long way and I only have my bicycle."

"I'll buy a car," de Gier said, "but it will be easier if you move in with me. You won't have to rush up and down all the time."

She kissed him back.

"I may, but this flat is awfully small for two people and two cats, and the cats won't like each other. It may be better if you move in with me."

"O.K.," de Gier said, "anything you say."

Esther stepped back. "Will you really give up your life here for me, Rinus? You are so comfortable in this flat. Won't it be better if I keep on coming here?"

"Marry me," de Gier said.

She giggled and pushed back her glasses, which had slipped down her nose.

"You're so old-fashioned, darling. Nobody wants to get married anymore these days. People live together now, haven't you noticed?"

"We'll have a child," de Gier said. "A son, or a daughter if you like. Twins, one of each."

"I'll think about it, dear, don't rush me. And I must go now. Did you have a pleasant day?"

"No."

"What happened?"

"Everything happened. I'll go with you. I can tell you about it in the bus. Leave your bicycle here. Then I'll be sure you're coming back."

She put Oliver down and de Gier picked him up, wrapping the cat around his neck and pulling its paws with both hands. Oliver yowled and tried to bite him but got his mouth full of hair and blew furiously.

"It's been a bad day," he said, "and I'll tell you all about it. But it will be the last time I ever tell you about my job. Police work should never be discussed."

"No, darling," she said as she brushed her hair.

"No, darling," he repeated and dropped Oliver, who forgot to turn over and landed on his side with a thud.

"Stupid cat," de Gier said.